TRINKETS

KIRSTEN SMITH

Little, Brown and Company
New York Boston

Copyright © 2013 by Kirsten Smith

Little, Brown and Company

Hachette Book Group
237 Park Avenue, New York, NY 10017
Visit our website at www.lb-teens.com

Little, Brown and Company is a division of Hachette Book Group, Inc.
The Little, Brown name and logo are trademarks of Hachette Book Group, Inc.

The publisher is not responsible for websites (or their content) that are not owned by the publisher.

First Edition: March 2013

Library of Congress Cataloging-in-Publication Data

Smith, Kirsten.
    Trinkets / by Kirsten Smith. — 1st ed.
        p. cm.
    Summary: When three Lake Oswego High School girls from different social groups, good-girl Elodie, popular Tabitha, and tough Moe, meet in a rehabilitation group, they discover they have much more in common than shoplifting.
    ISBN 978-0-316-16027-8
    [1. Interpersonal relations—Fiction.   2. Shoplifting—Fiction.
3. Rehabilitation—Fiction.   4. Conduct of life—Fiction.   5. High schools—
Fiction.   6. Schools—Fiction.   7. Family problems—Fiction.]   I. Title.
    PZ7.S6457Tri 2013
    [Fic]—dc23

                                                                        2012005477

10 9 8 7 6 5 4 3 2 1

RRD-C

Printed in the United States of America

To Hope Leon, partner in crime

SIZE:

PART ONE

5824583647 38824039

"Her low self-esteem is my good fortune."

This Must Be the Place

The people who say Portland is a place
where hipster thirtysomethings go to retire
clearly have never been to Lake Oswego,
my new hometown,
the burb of all burbs,
a suburban utopia of Audi-driving type As,
a place so white they call it "Lake No Negro,"
a place where dads go
when they don't care that their kid
was happier living in Idaho;
a place for dads to go when
they're hoping a constant downpour of rain
will wash away the past like it wasn't even there

and all they can see is a new job
and a pretty new wife
and a place
to send your daughter to be educated properly
and ignored resoundingly.

Old and New

Of the six months I've been here,
the first two were friendless
until I met Rachelle.
She needed a bestie and I needed *somebody*.
I met her by joining Yearbook,
which is a shortcut to friendship
if you're one of the new people.
I'm new enough so no one knows my name,
but I'm old enough to realize who everyone is.
I'm new enough not to understand
why they call Ken Headley "SpoogeBob,"
but I'm old enough to have heard that
Mr. Hart had to leave school
because he made a pass at Martin Pierce
in the bio lab.
I'm new enough to be clueless about
what the Interplanetary Analysis Club actually does,
but old enough to realize
if there's any guy
any girl
would kill to be with,
it's Brady Finch.

Human Anatomy

Brady is by his locker
and as he's reaching up to get something,
the word *sinew* comes to mind—
probably because we just learned it
in our human anatomy discussion in Biology.
I'm going to tell Mr. Lopez
that if he wants people
to really appreciate human anatomy,
he should show a slide of Brady Finch's forearm
while saying the word *sinew*
and I bet every girl's C-minus would
suddenly sprout into a B-plus.
Brady zips up his backpack
and slams his locker shut
and his sinew comes down
and curls around its rightful place in the world:
the shoulder of Tabitha Foster.

TABITHA

WHAT THE MIRROR SAYS

I wonder what the point of being quote-unquote popular is, since sometimes it's a highly annoying thing to be. For instance, idiots and plebeians constantly come up to you and invade your space with inane greetings, bids for attention, and pleas for friendship.

"Hey, Tabitha....How's it going?...Whassup?...Love your earrings...." Etc. Etc. Barf. Space invasions are draining.

Don't get me wrong. Of course I like it that people know me and I have the perks of getting away with whatever I want, but most of the time I would appreciate an iota of privacy.

Right now is one of the few times I actually receive said iota—hanging out in the bathroom with Kayla and Taryn. Sure, they talk about ridiculous things, but at least when they're looking in the mirror, they're not paying attention to me.

"I did an hour and a half of cardio last night," Kayla offers, pushing her long black hair out of her eyes. Asian girls are the luckiest when it comes to their hair. They barely have any on their bodies, and then they have these supershiny, hassle-free manes.

"I'm pretty sure Coke Zero makes you constipated," Taryn says, clutching her stomach.

A minute later Kayla squints at a bubbly blonde exiting the bathroom. "Serena Bell's on the Pill," she prattles. "That's why her boobs are so humongo."

"Mine are just a God-given gift," Taryn says, fluffing her cleavage out of her low-cut Juicy Couture top. It's true; her C-cups are an asset, and she sure as shit uses them as one.

For once Kayla and Taryn aren't barraging me with questions like "How's Brady?" and "What are we doing tonight?" because they're busy reapplying their makeup and primping and making faces at themselves in the mirror.

I'm a secret connoisseur of Mirror Faces. Every girl's is different. My mom's is a smoky glance, eyes half shut, all sexy and mysterious. Kayla puckers her lips like she's making a kiss, sucking in her cheeks. Taryn tilts her chin down, with a saucy little half smile, angled in a way so she looks ten pounds lighter. Too bad none of them can pull it off in real life. That's what sucks about a Mirror Face; you make it because it's how you want other people to see you, but you're the only person who actually gets to.

This is possibly a topic worthy of the LOHS blog, but who has time. Just because Ms. Hoberman gave me an A in Creative Writing last semester, it doesn't mean I should be wasting my time blogging. Blogging is for people who don't have social lives. Besides, Ms. Hoberman gives everybody an A. Hence, my signing up for her Shakespeare class this semester. The best thing is the field trips, where you get to hang out with your friends under the guise of extra credit. This year we only get a nighttime trip to Northwest Classical Theatre to see a play, but next year, when we're seniors, we go to Ashland for the weekend for the Shakespeare Festival. As in, an entire weekend where you get to hook up with your boyfriend and get drunk, and your parents foot the bill for the whole thing because they think you're "learning."

As for Brady, I've never seen his Mirror Face. His Everyday Face is pretty gorgeous, though. He has dimples and thick blond hair that he wears a little shaggy in the most adorable way, and he has moments of being truly charming. He's not a big believer in deep conversations, but what guy is? And really, what's the point? It's easier not to have deep conversations. You end up talking endlessly about your feelings, not his, and then exposing yourself too much until you finally arrive at a place of inevitable heartbreak and disappointment.

Kayla finishes putting on her opalescent pink Dior lip gloss complete with plumper. Her lips look blindingly sticky.

"Can we go?" I ask. Marcia Abrahams keeps looking

over at me, and I have a hunch she's gathering the courage to come over and ask me what I'm wearing to Spring Fling. She always asks me what I'm wearing, like clockwork, eleven weeks before a dance, and then somehow ends up wearing something almost identical. Imitation is supposed to be a compliment, but copycats are annoying and should be ignored whenever you see them plotting their space invasion.

That said, one advantage of being on a high rung of the Lakers social ladder is that you and your like-minded peers get to have your lockers right next to one another. I don't know how it happens that way, but it seems like the primo real estate always belongs to A-listers.

Kayla and Taryn and I saunter up to our bank of lockers to find Brady and his boys already there. Brady is getting a vitamin supplement out of his locker. He's very into "peak performance."

Jason Baines asks him, "Where were you last night?"

"Yeah," Noah Simos adds. "You never showed up at Ferber's."

"Didn't your mom tell you?" Brady says. "She had me come over to your house so she could suck my dick."

Have you ever noticed how boys love making jokes about sleeping with each other's mothers? Either that or discussing how gay the other person is. If you have a penis, you apparently possess an endless supply of this type of unfunny comedy.

Noah punches him, and Brady laughs, slinging his arm around me. I smell his D&G cologne. It isn't entirely unpleasant. I look up at him like, *You are the most charming person I know, and your arm around my shoulder makes me happier than anything in the entire world.*

"What time should I pick you up tonight?" he asks, kissing me.

"Like, nine?" I say. He may be kind of a D-bag, but he does have nice lips. And he's six two, which is good, since I'm an inch or so taller than most of the girls in my grade. Sometimes people ask if I've ever modeled. My mom took me to get professionally photographed once, but I hated it. It was all hot lights and faking it, and it got boring fast. Although, in a weird way, I guess you could say that's what I'm doing now, looking up at Brady and playing the part of Perfect Girlfriend. Either that or I'm giving him my very own Mirror Face.

*MOE

FEBRUARY 19

I know I wasn't directly responsible for Lindsay Manatore having to run track with one half sweatpants, one half short shorts, but I probably should have stopped Alex from cutting the leg off them with Janet's pocketknife. But in a way I'm glad I didn't, because it was funny. Anytime we crossed Lindsay's path on the track, I would start to sing, "Who wears short shorts?"

Alex befriended me in the first place because she thinks I'm funny. That, and she assumed because I dress the way I do, I belonged in their social circle. I told her, "Oh no, I just have a terrible fashion sense." Next thing I know, I was being introduced by Alex to her friends as her hilarious, sarcastic new friend Moe. That was at the beginning of freshman year, and that's the person I've stayed ever since. Before that, I was friends with losers, but I've got to say being with the tough kids or the "burnouts" or whatever you'd call them has its perks because no one effs with you. The problem is people mostly avoid you because they assume you're dangerous or you'll beat the crap out of them, so you don't really have a chance to mingle a whole lot.

The only person who sees something close to the real me is Noah. He probably would not admit that in HIS journal. But he's a popular kid, and those kids don't even keep journals. Their lives revolve around status updates, and by status I mean STATUS. He hangs out with people like Tabitha Foster and Brady Finch and Jason Baines. Noah only talks to me after school when we're alone, then he leaves before my aunt gets back from work. Or I leave before his mom gets home.

Yesterday I waved at him when I saw him walking into his house with his parents. He didn't wave back. I heard his mom say, "Who's that?" His response: "I don't know." Hey, asshole, if you're going to pretend not to know me, that's fine, but I live next door to you. Couldn't you just say, "I think she lives next door to us"? I don't need him to pro-claim undying love for me or tell the whole world that we make out and sometimes do even more than that, but at least admit I'm a person you're familiar with. Douche.

TABITHA

GOOD BODY IMAGE

"Please tell me it's not gonna rain later." Kayla points, looking at the gray sky as we walk up the perfectly manicured walkway to Taryn's front door.

"Sorry. It's gonna rain later," I say. It's Portland. It rains 155 days a year.

Kayla rings the bell, which echoes out some cathedral-on-crack-style chimes. The house is a gaudy white McMansion perched right on the water in Lake Oswego. Not my taste, but in our neighborhood new money reigns supreme, and this is the perfect example of what it buys you. Taryn's parents have oodles of fresh cash, courtesy of her dad's sweet upper-management job at Nike and her mom's at Wieden+Kennedy.

"I'll drive," Taryn offers, tossing her curly blond hair as she swings open the front door.

"I want to find something *hot*," Kayla says, fingering her belly-button ring, which is proudly on display thanks to a strategically rolled-up sweatshirt, designed to show off her lean, flat stomach.

Kayla has a gym in her house, and she wears a red rubber "core bracelet" on her wrist to remind her to suck in her stomach. Her personal hero is Tracy Anderson, Gwyneth Paltrow's trainer. I'm pretty sure she owns Tracy's entire workout wardrobe, down to the shoes. If her mom would let her, she'd probably dye her hair blond to match Tracy's, but fortunately she realized that "blond Asian" is not the greatest look. Thanks, Bai Ling.

We reach Taryn's red Mini, a present from her parents for the incredible accomplishment of turning sixteen. Kayla crawls into the backseat.

"Don't you already have a closet full of hot?" I nudge her.

"Too much is never enough," she singsongs.

Our Friday afternoon shopping excursions are a ritual. I used to love them, but then about a year ago, I started wondering if spending my dad's cash was just another form of taking his hush money; if he didn't have so much of it, my mom probably would have divorced him a long time ago. Every time I buy something with a fifty-dollar bill he's given me, I'm going into greater debt with the enemy. But if it weren't for the enemy, I guess I wouldn't have gotten Tiffany diamond-stud earrings for Christmas last year.

We peel into the Washington Square parking lot, and Taryn does one of her typical "I need two spaces instead of one" parking jobs, nearly plowing into a guy in a wheel-chair.

"Jesus!" I yell.

"Just because he's handicapped doesn't mean you need to put him out of his misery," Kayla adds.

"Whatever. He'd thank me for it if he knew Macy's doesn't carry Miu Miu," Taryn sniffs. She is one of those girls who live for any razzle-dazzle chance at fashionista-dom and the possibility of possessing couture. Not that the Washington Square Mall is crawling with couture, but you'd be surprised at how many kids in our grade have dads with Learjets and moms who still trot out furs for parent-teacher meetings. If anyone can sniff out a thousand-dollar dress in a mall, Taryn can. She once used the bio lab tables as an impromptu fashion runway when Mr. Lopez left the room for one of his infamous fifteen-minute bathroom breaks.

Kayla starts gravitationally beelining toward Forever 21, the home of all her slut-wear. "Let's go to Forever Twenty-One," she says.

"We're going to Bebe," Taryn says firmly. Spring Fling is almost three months away, but she's hell-bent on nabbing the perfect dress early.

"Why do you want to go to Forever Twenty-One? They print Bible verses on the bottoms of their shopping bags." I roll my eyes.

"They do not!" Kayla gasps.

"See for yourself," I say with a shrug. "I'm going to Nordie's." I suggest it because I know neither of them will want to go there. It's "too nineties."

"Meet back at Yopop for fro-yo afterward?" Taryn says, and I nod.

Kayla points at the Forever 21 window. "Ooh—glitter tube top!"

"Watch out," I say. "Total sinner wear. You might need some redemption."

Kayla sticks out her tongue, and I can't help but laugh. She may be a bit of a ludicrous idiot, but she's at least somewhat trustworthy. When I drunkenly told her about my dad having an affair last year, she never mentioned it again. And in exchange, I never talk about all the slutty things she's done with half the guys she's done them with. Last year in Family and Consumer Science (formerly known as Home Ec), Mrs. Sykes talked about a study where girls who had good body image were more likely to abstain from sex, and girls with bad body image were more likely to be promiscuous. How weird is it that if you like your body, you don't let anyone see it, and if you *don't* like your body, you want to show it to everyone? And why wouldn't Kayla love her body, since there isn't an ounce of fat on it?

"See you in forty-five minutes," Tayrn says. As they head off, I breathe a sigh of relief. I can finally do what I came here to do.

*MOE

FEBRUARY 24

Marc and I played Rage after school. Beached Whales were exploding left and right when he started giving me shit because I hang out with dirtbags and a guy who doesn't even acknowledge me in public. I told him I don't need his overprotective brother speech. It's not like his friends are a ton better, since all they do is blaze up and ride bikes. He argued with me for a while and said that's different from actually doing bad things like tagging buildings or being mean to people or constantly partying and whatever else we do. I said it's none of his business what we do, and besides, who else am I supposed to hang out with? So he let it drop and said he's just looking out for me, and then he killed a shit ton of Gingers and Fattys. I was pissed until I realized that's just what brothers do. They try to protect you from the bad guys, even in a video game.

TABITHA

CHARMED

Even if you have enough money to do what you want, it's still fun trying to get something for free. Especially something from the Nordie's jewelry case.

"Can I see that one?" I ask, pointing to a Maya Brenner bracelet with chunky gold chains and a little coin with small stones of turquoise and coral. The other day I saw Alexa Chung wearing it on a blog.

The despondent saleslady unlocks the case. She looks like all the gloomy weather has soaked straight through to her soul. Either that or she's been sprayed with a little too much Eau de Homeless on her walk to work. That could bum out anybody.

"Oh, and the earrings," I say once she plunks the charm bracelet on the velvet pad on the counter. She turns to get them.

"No, not those." I point. "The pearl ones. And that silver bracelet with the big chain links? And can I see the gold hoops? Thanks so much." As the saleswoman sets out one thing after another, I smile sweetly. "Do you mind getting out that pendant necklace too? Sorry."

"Which one?" She's starting to get confused.

"It's so hard to make up my mind here," I say, holding up the gold hoops. "By the way, I love your blouse. It looks amazing on you."

"It does?" She looks down at her navy-blue sheath as if seeing herself for the first time. I feel a little guilty for preying on her insecurities, but I guess on the plus side she looks happier now than she did five minutes ago.

"Jean, there's someone on line three for you—Eric?" a woman from the Clinique counter calls over.

From the look on Jean's face, it's obvious Eric has been dodging her for weeks. His favorite activities are probably Nintendo, drinking Coors, and not returning the calls of women he's had sex with. Jean is obviously one of them. Seeing her happy face, I remember feeling that excited when Brady used to call me. Now I just feel stuck in a loop of bad chitchat and sloppy make-out sessions. Sometimes, yes, we do the actual deed, but we're usually drunk, so I don't even know if it qualifies. It's basically a formula of grabs, gropes, and insertions, all leading to an inevitably brief conclusion. I wouldn't rank it as one of my all-time favorite activities. This trip to the mall would score way higher.

"I'm with a customer. Tell him I'll call him back," Jean says, casting a disappointed eye my way.

"No, it's cool." I give her a knowing smile. "Go ahead. I'm fine."

"I'll be right back." Jean nods appreciatively and goes to take the call. Jackpot.

"Hey, stranger!" Jean blurts into the phone. After a second she says, "Yeah, I love Ruth's Chris!..." Then her shoulders slump. "I think I still have it. It was only a fifty-dollar gift certificate, though, so I'm not sure how big a dinner it will get us...."

He wants her to take him out to dinner with *her* gift certificate? Jesus. Jean needs to hang up on this guy and delete his number. But whatever—her low self-esteem is my good fortune. When she hangs up, I give her a little wave and say, "Thanks! I'll come back later!" and stroll off. Leaving everything behind but the Maya Brenner bracelet.

BRILLIANT CON ARTIST

Walking your trinket out of the store is the worst and best part. You're about to become either a brilliant con artist or another juvenile-delinquency statistic.

I force myself to slow down and supposedly admire a pink sundress, but underneath the sleeve of my sweater, I'm covertly ripping off the price tag and tiny bar-code sensor from the bracelet, which is fastened on my wrist. I drop the tag and sensor on the floor and walk on through Sporting Goods.

Ninety seconds later, I'm at the street exit. I take a deep breath and make the final plunge through the electronic gates by the front doors—which, 87 percent of the time, are for show, but still they're the final, exhilaratingly scary hurdle—and I push open the door. The winter air hits me like a slap of freedom.

I quicken my pace as I start toward the parking lot. I figure I'll make a hard right in thirty feet, walk around the building, and reenter the mall near Yopop. I pull out my phone to text Kayla my ETA, and move faster and faster, freer and freer. I pick up speed and round the corner of the building, and that's when I walk right smack into a security guard.

CAUGHT

Blood bolts to the surface of my skin so hard it feels like my face is being pricked by a hundred little pins.

I have no freaking clue what to do, so I cover. Badly. "Oops. Sorry. I'm such a spaz—"

He smiles a slow, casual smile. A tattoo of a bobcat or some kind of jungle lion peeks out from under his collar. I stare at it. Was he my age when he decided to permanently ink himself? Was it something he did with his friends? I wonder if he regrets it.

"I'll need you to come with me," he says.

"Why?"

He chuckles a little bit. "I think you know."

"I do?" I ask. There is literally no oxygen going in or out of my body.

"Girls who steal three-hundred-dollar bracelets aren't as dumb as they look."

"I didn't steal anything." I try to make my Mirror Face, my model face, my "you are the most charming person I know, and your arm around my shoulder makes me happier than anything in the entire world" face, but he doesn't buy it.

"I need you to come back inside and show me what's on your wrist."

I have no choice. So I say, "Oh, shit! Is this what you're talking about?" I hold out my wrist. "I totally forgot I tried it on! I'm an idiot."

He smiles at me. Just beneath his smile, I can see the tattooed point of the bobcat's claw, poised above his jugular.

"You may have 'forgotten'"—he stresses the word, obviously not believing me—"but you still left the store without paying for it, which means you broke the law."

When we head back inside, I try to look like nothing's wrong, but then I see Jean standing there by the big glass doors. She's pointing me out to her coworker and wearing a smug smile on her face. Ten minutes ago, Jean was the loser and I was the winner. Now it's a completely different story.

"Eric is just using you for a free steak," I snipe to Jean as we pass. Her smug smile disappears. The guard holds out his arm for me to take, and it's almost the way a gentleman leads a lady onto the dance floor—or a bobcat drags its prey into the forest after the chase is over.

SIZE:

PART
TWO

5824583647 38824039

"This is what happens to princesses in real life."

MARCH 2

Okay, question of the day: What's the big deal about Spring Fling? People blow hundreds of dollars on one night for a cheesy photo with a backdrop full of stars. I'll admit the prospect of dancing to pop songs with Noah Simos isn't the worst thing I can imagine, but it's never actually going to happen, so there's no use wasting time thinking about it.

Aunt B keeps telling me stories about her high school dances, which are fully boring. She keeps insisting that if I don't go to Spring Fling I'll regret it. She's big on "living life to the fullest" and having "no regrets." I always feel that's what people who peaked in high school say. Not that it's her fault—she didn't plan on having to give up her life because my parents died in a random accident and she had to become guardian. Of course I have regrets, like not paying more attention to my folks when they were right in front of me, but I try not to spend too much time dwelling on it, because I was only seven when it happened. I have a few special memories I keep to myself and a few things I wish I'd done differently, like not whining about wanting a skateboard for my birthday. If I hadn't, they probably would still be alive. But the more you think about stuff like that, the worse you feel, and the more you talk about special memories, the less special they become. Marc and I actually agree on this topic, and last year for Christmas, he gave Aunt B a T-shirt that says "No Regrets" as a kind of joke. She didn't laugh. He said he regretted giving it to her, but she didn't laugh at that either.

Small Talk

When I get home,
I give my dad the permission slip
for the Shakespeare field trip.
If you go,
you're a shoo-in for the Ashland overnight trip,
which is supposed to be the most fun
you can have in school
and still get credit for it.
He asks me how school is
and how my friends are.
I tell him *fine* and he nods and says,
*I'm available to problem-solve if you're having any
    difficulties, Elodie,*
and he gives me one of his District Manager Looks,
which makes me think I should

be paying him a salary for talking to me.
Maybe he should bill me after dinner.

As she's clearing the plates
my stepmom, Jenna, reminds me they're going to the
     Stegemans' later.
She's stoked at the prospect of small-talking herself into a
     stupor.
That's one of her special skills:
saying a whole lot of nothing
all the time.
I guess my dad married her because
silent types like people
who aren't silent.

What are you and Rachelle up to tonight? Jenna asks.
I shrug and say, *Nothing, probably just watching movies,*
because that's the way it is with parents;
you tell them what they want to hear
and everything else
you leave out.

TABITHA

ICE

After Mr. Bobcat calls the police, my mother shows up, pale-faced and with her usually perfectly coiffed ash-blond hair mussed up on the sides. Clearly, she was in the middle of a cocktail–fueled power nap.

But I have to hand it to her—she barely flinches when she sees me sitting in the dank little chair in the back of the Customer Service Center.

On the drive home, she calls Jeffrey, an attorney and "old family friend," on speakerphone. They went to college together at UW, and once when I asked her if they ever dated, she just shrugged it off. Two Christmases ago at our house, I walked in on them having drinks in the kitchen. He was telling her a story that had her doubled over laughing, which is weird because she's not really a big laugher.

When she saw me, she straightened up and tried to collect herself, but he just stood there staring at her, like he wished he could live in that kitchen forever and not have to go home with his plus-sized wife and their super-annoying five-year-old twin sons.

Apparently, my mom's already given Jeffrey the lowdown, because he comes on the speakerphone full of confidence and calm. "I'll handle the paperwork," he says. "I've had my assistant enroll you in a counseling rehabilitation program."

"I'm going to *rehab*?"

"You need to show the judge you're addressing your problem," he says.

"I don't have a problem." I roll my eyes.

"I'll e-mail your mom the information."

"What if I don't want to go to a program? I've never been arrested before. It's not like they're going to send me to jail if I don't go to a program, right?"

"Actually, the state's been cracking down on shoplifters. Statistically, thirty-five percent of first-offender shoplifters are high-risk repeaters. If we show them you aren't one of the thirty-five percent, we have more ammo to plea-bargain," he says.

"She'll do it," my mom interjects. "We really appreciate all your help, Jeffrey." She grips the steering wheel tightly and shoots me a sharp glance. "Don't we?"

I don't answer. Plea-bargain? Please. I took one tiny little bracelet. It's not like I'm Winona Ryder.

*   *   *

When we get home, my mom goes into the living room, smooths her dress, and sits on the arm of a plum-colored Barcelona chair—a new addition, thanks to her latest renovation.

The clink of ice cubes in my mom's glass is the only sound in the house, other than the distant hum of an ever-present mower two houses down. Mr. Patterson apparently thinks if he mows his yard morning, noon, and night into pure perfection, then somehow maybe his life will improve. He's obviously delusional.

I fiddle with my phone. There are eight texts from Kayla and Taryn, asking WHERE THE HELL DID U GO? I can't exactly say the truth, so I write SORRY. PMS CU @ PARTY.

My mother takes another sip of her drink—"club soda," aka straight Tanqueray.

"I still do not understand *why* you would shoplift." She sighs.

I look away. "I told you—it was a stupid misunderstanding."

"Your dad or I could have given you money to buy that bracelet."

"I'm sorry, all right?" I say. It seems to satisfy her, especially because she prefers easy explanations to life's complicated problems.

"Jeffrey says that program is only for twelve weeks," she says. "He thinks if you have good attendance, you can

33

get it taken off your record altogether. He didn't want me to tell you that, though. He thinks scaring you might be a good thing." She shoots me a look, furrowing her brow as much as her Botox allows. Then she adds, "I'm not telling your father about this. He doesn't need the stress."

Duh. Who *needs* the stress of their kid getting busted for stealing? She goes to refill her drink, and I stand up. I can't take this conversation anymore. I need to go do what I do best, which is get dressed and make myself pretty so I can go to a party with a bunch of people I can't stand.

What We're Doing

Derek Godfrey—
whoever he is—
is having a party
and we're going.
It's the first party I've been to in Oregon,
or maybe it's my first party ever, really,
aside from a birthday here and there.
That kind of sums me up:
I'm here and there but not really anywhere.

I'm only here now because I'm Rachelle's plus one,
a beta to her alpha.
That was the unspoken agreement, anyway;
if she deigned to take me under her wing,

I'd do whatever she said,
no questions asked.
Tonight she claims I need to get some candids for
   Yearbook,
so I'd better bring my camera.

When I get to her house,
she's wearing a teeny bit too much makeup
and a skirt that's supershort
and a wide-eyed look that says,
If I don't have a good time tonight,
I'll DIE.
Proving that even alphas get nervous
here and there.

*MOE

MARCH 7

Staying in and writing in my journal is not what people would expect someone like me to do on a Friday night. Troublemakers like me smash mailboxes on Friday nights. Burnouts like me get baked on Friday nights. Tough girls like me do not explore their feelings on Friday nights.

When Noah told me that he was going to Derek's party tonight, a part of me—ALL of me—was disappointed. Sometimes I wish I could just morph into a cheerleader or whatever I'd need to be to make Noah feel comfortable being seen together. But even in my dreamworld, that cheerleading uniform looks itchy and uncomfortable.

Obviously, I can't tell anyone I want to be at Derek's party. And doing mushrooms with Alex and Janet and those guys at the Oaks Amusement Park sounds lame, so that's why I'm here.

Marc is out playing video games at the Avalon in SE. My aunt is out to dinner with her friends from the hospital. I'm glad, because she never goes out; it's like she feels too guilty or stressed to have fun. She always does her best to make sure Marc and I are taken care of: She makes us breakfast, eats dinner with us, asks us how our days were, follows up on our schoolwork, and is generally concerned about us. She's older than my parents were, and she says it's crazy that they died when they were young and in love and had a family, and she was single and older. I know this sounds bad, but I feel like she should try to get over it. That's what we're trying to do. That's why it's good she's out having fun and drinking white wine or whatever ladies her age drink. Maybe she'll flirt with a nice forty-something guy. I'm going to use this opportunity to take a relaxing bubble bath and read. Like I said, not what people would expect, but all in all not a bad way to spend a Friday night if you can't spend it with the person you love.

Normal Teenage Girl

The second Rachelle and I get to Derek Godfrey's,
I wish I was somewhere else.
It makes me feel like a freak,
because doesn't every normal teenage girl
love going to parties?
I must not be normal.

Then I see Brady Finch walk in.
Even if he's out of my league,
I still think it's better
having a crush on someone who's awesome but
    unattainable
than having a crush on

someone gettable and lame.
At least I have standards.

He walks by
and jostles my arm
and turns and says, *Excuse me, sweetie.*
Sweetie?! Brady Finch just called me *sweetie*?
As I stand there in the wake of his glow,
some drunk guy says to me,
What are you smiling about?
and hands me a pink drink in a red cup.
Nothing, I say, blushing.
Maybe you'll be more fun after you're drunk, he says,
    and staggers off.
Rachelle appears beside me, all sympathetic, and
    says,
That guy's a dick. We can go if you want to.
I have a pang of affection for her,
because even though she's not the bestest bestie in
    the world,
she's the only one I've got.

I'm gonna say bye to Samantha first,
she says, pointing to a group of cheerleaders,
and I glance over at Brady and see
that now he's surrounded by people.
I head outside,
chugging a sip of night air
like it's something that will make me happy

and drunk and
I'll forget where I am
or who I am
or how badly I suck
at being normal.

TABITHA

DEREK'S PARTY

Derek's house is a five-bedroom affair that sits atop Westridge Estates. It's famous for its sweet pool table, bought by Derek's divorced dad, who's always out of town with younger girls he's trying to impress.

When I get there, I'm greeted with the sight of a hammered Jenny Heder and Serena Bell rapping along to Kanye blasting out of a huge sound system. I love how hip-hop is the voice of white-girl suburban angst. Derek's dad works at Adidas, making him single *and* loaded, so he's tricked out the house with speakers and games and is so desperate for his son to love him that he tells him it's okay to have parties when he's gone. Mix that with Jason Baines having an older brother who buys him booze in bulk, and you've got a winning combination of party possibilities.

I make a quick detour into the kitchen to retrieve an

extremely crappy strawberry daiquiri from Patrick Cushman, who's apparently appointed himself Blender Master.

"Special recipe created for teenagers who want to get drunk quick," he says.

"How'd *you* get put in charge of cocktails?"

"Does it matter?"

I shrug. Patrick is one of those guys who don't seem to belong to any group; he always floats along with everyone—tennis players, smart kids, band geeks, skaters—and sometimes he even hangs out with Brady's lacrosse friends. It probably means he's insecure and can't decide who he is. We had freshman gym together. One day some asshole pegged me really hard in dodgeball, and Patrick walked me to the nurse's office to get an ice pack for my arm. He was obviously creeping on me, but it wasn't bad to have the company.

I take a giant chug of daiquiri. It's strong and sweet and sour. The taste makes me pucker.

"You must really want to get drunk, huh?" he says.

"None of your business." I glare at him.

"Whoa. Sorry," he says, looking taken aback.

"Whatever." I don't need his pity. I leave him standing there and head for the living room, taking another glug of daiquiri as I go. He may be annoying to talk to, but I have to admit, Patrick Cushman does make a pretty delicious, extremely crappy strawberry daiquiri.

"Hey, Tabs," Brady says, smirking at me as I walk up and say hi to everyone. Taryn's too busy texting to say hi back.

Brady puts an arm around my waist and pinches the spot where a teeny bit of flesh bubbles out over my jeans. I'm only a size 6, but clearly this is his way of telling me I'm fat. Sometimes it seems like guys really hate girls, with all the little things they say and do to try to get us to hate ourselves.

I fight the urge to hit him and instead turn and plant a kiss on his perfect mouth. I've seen my mom do it to my dad when he's being a dick. She tries to trick him with affection into being in a good mood. Sometimes it even works.

"Where did you go earlier?" Taryn asks, looking up from her phone.

"Cabbed it home," I say with a shrug.

"You could have texted us. We sat at Yopop for twenty minutes waiting for you," she gripes.

"Like I have to broadcast everywhere I am at all times?" I snap. I mouth *cramps* to Kayla. Any explanation involving people's periods works for Kayla. She got hers late—she was fourteen, which is practically menopausal—so she loves stories about the follies of menstruation. Her favorite is one about her cousin's first attempt at wearing a maxi pad. Her cousin got her period in the middle of a family Christmas party, so someone gave her a pad. She came out of the bathroom looking tragically uncomfortable.

"What's wrong?" Kayla asked when her cousin waddled over like she had on a diaper full of fire ants. Her cousin pointed to her crotch and whispered to Kayla, "Sticky side up, right?"

Brady lets go of my waist. "We're going to Jason's for an after-party. You ready?"

I stare at him. "I just got here."

"So?"

"So, I haven't even finished my drink." I hold up my daiquiri as proof, then look at his perfect mouth, which I once again want to punch.

"So? Finish it in the car."

I stare at Brady. How did I end up with a boyfriend like this? A boyfriend whose talents are scoring points in lacrosse, monitoring my body fat, and being a dick. He knows I don't like Jason Baines. I've told him that a hundred times. I don't like this Jason or any Jason. "Jason" is the universal moniker of assholes. I've never met one who's cool. And this particular one—with his jock complex and his self-absorbed, IQ-limited girlfriend, Dakota—is definitely *not* cool. I see the night unfolding exactly as every night with Jason unfolds: Brady and Jason staying up until four in the morning, getting drunker and drunker and stupider and stupider, and me sitting there talking to Dakota. Who, by the way, has been known to make racial slurs when she's hammered. Sometimes I wish I could kidnap her and drop her smack-dab in the middle of Felony Flats in the middle of the night and see how far her mouth gets her.

Brady knows how I feel, but he's decided to trap me into going to Jason's by suggesting it in front of ten other people; if I say no, I'll look like a bitch. As of right now, he's winning this battle. I gulp my daiquiri.

"Can I talk to you in private for a second?" I say, fake-smiling.

"We can talk on the way. Right, guys?" He grins at the guys and then turns back to me with an even smugger smile.

"I'm not going." I glare at him.

"Oh, really?"

"Yep."

"Typical," he sneers.

Kayla shoots Noah a look. Jason gloats. Dakota looks bored.

"What do you mean, 'typical'?" I retort.

"You're making a big deal out of nothing. Typical."

"Fuck you," I blurt.

Everyone starts to look uncomfortable now. Because of all the people who'd be fighting at a party in front of everyone, it shouldn't be me and Brady Finch. We're supposed to be this awesome prince and princess of the high school, two people who look great together and are madly in love.

"I kind of wish you'd pull that giant stick out of your ass," he says.

Brady and Jason and Noah all laugh. Kayla doesn't look at me. Suddenly, I don't want to punch him anymore. I just want to run away. I'm hit with the realization that this is what happens to princesses in real life. They don't get kissed awake by princes. They don't get handed the keys to the kingdom. They don't live happily ever after. In real life, they are publicly humiliated; they are thrown from their towers. This is what they don't tell you when you are a little girl: Everyone secretly hates a princess. Everyone wants to see her fall.

Feeling sick to my stomach, I turn and walk out, pawing my way through the party like a newly crowned pariah. Finally I walk out the front door of Derek Godfrey's house, fighting the overwhelming feeling that if I keep going, I'm on my own now, and I'm on my own for good.

On the Porch

I'm on the porch,
still holding the drink
the drunk guy gave me,
when someone smashes into me
and my cup goes flying.
I turn to see Tabitha Foster,
her white shirt dripping with pink drink.
She is lean and mean,
all honey hair and devil-may-care.
She is nothing like you, and she is nothing like me.
Of all the queens of all the schools I've been to,
there's something ultra-something
about Tabitha Foster.
She looks like she's stepping

out of a movie
or a dream
or a story that
has a happy ending—
except, apparently,
for this one.

TABITHA

HANDKERCHIEF

"Son of a *bitch*!" I yell.

I'm drenched in daiquiri, spilled on me by a girl who looks vaguely familiar, with wavy brown hair and a slim build, wearing jeans and a lavender sweater. Basically, she looks like every other girl at LO: utterly, blandly normal.

"Oh! Are you okay?" She dabs at my tight white Vanessa Bruno shirt with regret. I stole it six days ago, and tonight was the first night I wore it. Now it's coated in sticky pink ick. Thanks, bitch.

I hear somebody cackle, and I look back over my shoulder into the house, where Brady and Jason are staring at me. Dakota has her hand over her mouth. A pang of rage zips through me.

I spin back around and snarl at the girl. "Why don't you watch where the hell you're going?!"

"I'm—sorry," she stammers. "I know people always say they're sorry when they don't really mean it, but I'm not one of them. Although—I guess there are some people who don't say it at all, so maybe it's better to be someone who says it but doesn't mean it...." She trails off.

I stare at her. Seriously? She's choosing to embark on a weird theory about apologies on Derek Godfrey's porch right now?

The girl digs into her coat pocket for a second and then says, "Here. Use this."

She holds out a small, folded square piece of cotton. It's lacy and yellow. I yank it out of her hand and mop my shirt with it.

"You carry this for times when you spill shit all over people?" I snark. Then I realize how bitchy I sound. It's not this idiot's fault I'm in a bad mood. I curse the security guard at Nordstrom and low-self-esteem Jean and my wet shirt and Brady Finch and my whole life, before taking a breath. "Sorry," I mutter.

The girl looks at me for a second, then says, "See? You just did it."

"What?"

"Said you're sorry and didn't mean it," the girl says. She grabs her yellow handkerchief out of my hand and walks off down the driveway and into the night.

Leaves & Branches

It's starting to drizzle
as I cut through someone's side yard
beginning to bloom with spring flowers.
Eminem's "Not Afraid"
thumps at my back as
I beeline toward Rachelle's house.
I've always had a good sense of direction;
my mom said it was one of the gifts
I got from my dad and not from her.
She was always going on about how alike
we were,
probably because she knew we weren't.
How could we be?
My dad specializes in strategic planning,
and I just not-so-strategically
insulted one of the most popular girls in school.

I call Rachelle and she answers,
sounding like she's in the middle of riding a roller coaster.
I think I'm gonna stay awhile! she yells.
I thought you weren't having any fun, I say.
She covers the mouthpiece for a second,
then says, *AwmwichJamminjeeyaz!*
What? I say, and she hisses,
I said, I'm with Dustin Diaz!
Who's that? I say.
Wait—he's going downstairs! Call you tomorrow—

With that, she hangs up on me.
The rain starts to come down harder,
and I duck underneath a big elm tree
that has probably been giving out shade and oxygen
for the last fifty years.
I realize the thing
about friends you've only had for four months
is that they aren't going to stand over you
and protect you with their branches
and photosynthesize carbon dioxide for you;
they aren't going to shelter you from the sun
and shield you from the rain;
they're going to throw you over
for a guy they barely know
as you stand there getting wetter
and wetter.

*MOE

MARCH 8, 4:22 A.M.!!

I got woken up by Noah knocking on my window. He said
he left the party because "it was boring without you there." I
thought it was just the alcohol talking, that he just wanted to
hook up before passing out, but then he actually started telling me about his night. He told me Brady Finch is kind of a
dick and one time pissed in Patrick Cushman's locker for no
reason. He said Patrick is a guy who's never done anything
dicky to anybody. It confirmed my suspicions that I wouldn't
want to be friends with those types of people. That is, if they
ever even tried to talk to me. Although maybe my friends are
just as bad, who knows. None of us are perfect, I guess. Anyway, I kept waiting for him to lean over and kiss me, but
instead we talked until he fell asleep mid-sentence, and I'm
writing this now as he sleeps. He snores a little bit, which is
kind of adorable.

Mush

I hate breakfast.
Especially when it's oatmeal and especially
when I have to listen to Jenna's review
of her night at the Stegemans':
how nice everyone was
and how much fun they had
and what a great neighborhood this is
and how happy she is we moved here.
We heard from one of the parents
you kids had a party last night?
she says, all coy. *Did you go?*
I grunt a nonresponse
and cram a spoonful of wet oats
into my mouth.
She looks at my dad and smirks.

I guess we don't get to hear all the juicy details, do we, Ray?
She leans over to kiss him,
which is so not what you
want to see at nine in the morning:
your dad and stepmom making out.

Fortunately, my dad says
he has a big presentation on Monday
and he needs to go get ready for it,
which makes sense because
he's not really one for public speaking,
but I still wish that didn't require him
to get up and leave me sitting there alone
eating mush and blueberries
with the secretary
he married.

TABITHA

ROMANTIC HISTORY

My parents met when my mom was just out of college and working as an assistant for an interior design firm in Seattle. Her company was brought in to design one of my dad's office buildings, a six-story building on Pike Street. He was a brash associate architect then, and after a few weeks of flirting, he asked her out for a drink. She wasn't sure she should go, because she was still half seeing her college boyfriend, but she figured this was work and what could one drink hurt? So he took her to the top of the Space Needle for gin gimlets, which she'd never had before. Two of those turned into four, and as the story goes, they stayed for a five-hour dinner, talking and laughing and requesting bad seventies songs like "The Piña Colada Song" from the piano player, who thought they were charming. At the end of the night, my dad drove her home and shook her hand like a gentleman. She thought that must mean he didn't like her as much as she liked him or he was dating someone else. But he kept finding excuses to show up, even though his work on the building was basically done. He claimed it was his responsibility to "oversee" everything down to the very last detail, and she didn't argue, but she kept her distance. On the night before the building opened, everyone was toasting with champagne, and he introduced her to his boss as "the woman I'm going to marry." She thought he was joking and said, "We've only gone out once. How could you say that?" And apparently he responded, "Once was all it took," or something cheesy like that. But I guess she didn't think it was cheesy, because she got married to him three months later. They were so in love, they had a baby eight months after they got married, causing anyone with half a brain to realize there was some sort of miscalculation in terms of either birth control or logical thinking.

Now a couple of decades have passed, and my dad's off working in the living room, and my mom is on the phone with my older brother, Jake, who goes to the University of Michigan. I'm sitting on the couch watching a lame movie on TNT and listening to my mom laugh at all of Jake's stupid jokes. The way she used to laugh at my dad's, which makes sense, since Jake's basically a clone of my dad.

"Lemme talk to Jake," my dad calls out, and my mother reluctantly crosses to the dining room to hand over the phone. She says, "I love you so much, Jake," and for a second I get confused because my dad's name is Jacob, and I sometimes remember her calling my dad "Jake" and my brother "Jakey." So for a second I think she's saying "I love you" to my dad. Which would make zero sense.

"Hey, bud," my dad says, and launches into bro code with my brother as my mom disappears upstairs. Men sometimes talk to each other in these fake voices, like they're weird androids without feelings or emotions, and say words like *buddy* and *dude*.

Just then I get a text from Taryn: WHAT HAPPENED TO U LAST NITE?

I type back: I WAS ANNOYED.

That seems like as good an answer as any, and I go back to what I was watching on TNT. It's an old Sandra Bullock movie, one where she meets her dream guy on the Internet and falls in love with him, but it turns out he's a total asshole and then he ruins her life. I wonder if my mom's ever seen this one.

MARCH 8, 9:32 A.M.

I'm really glad Aunt B didn't walk into my room this morning to wake me up like she normally does. She would have been pretty pissed to see Noah Simos in my bed. It was weird to open my eyes this morning and see him staring right back at me. He kissed me good-bye, which was nice but I wish I'd had a chance to brush my teeth first. It sucks to be ignored by him sometimes, but when we're together he's so sweet I almost forget about everything else.

He climbed out the window when he heard Aunt B, and she didn't notice anything was up at breakfast. I arranged my eggs and bacon into a smiley face that looked like Noah, but Marc walked by and messed it up with his fork, so I had to punch him. Aunt B yelled at me, which was okay because I was in such a good mood that I apologized immediately and told her she was a very smart lady, so she went off to work in high spirits, feeling like I respected her, which could only be considered a banner way to start the day.

Stolen Goods

There's a guy in the Hair Care section of Fred Meyer
who's looking at me like he knows
what kind of person I am.
Then I realize I'm being paranoid.
There's no way he—or anyone, for that matter—
could know I'm the kind of person who has
three lip glosses,
a Hello Kitty alarm clock,
a packet of Red Vines,
a box of condoms (so I can see what they look like up close),
and a box of Crayola markers
in my bag.
To top it all off,
I slip a rhinestone barrette in there too,
one that Rachelle might like.

Nothing helps new friendships like surprise trinkets.
Fortunately, Rachelle knows my parents have money,
so she'll never guess her gifts are stolen,
but if she were a thief herself,
she'd understand that a stolen present
means way more than one that's been bought,
because of what you had to go through to get it.

Out the Door

I walk out the door,
past the guy collecting money
for some charitable cause or other,
and I give him a dollar
and a good-girl smile,
and that's when I feel
a hand
on my shoulder.
I'm gonna need you to come back into the store.
I turn around and there's the creepy guy from Hair Care,
and next to him is the nice old lady
from the candy aisle.
What's wrong? I say.
And the nice old lady says,
We need to see what's in your bag.
For a sick second,
I'm happy
because someone realizes I'm not just a good girl
or some stupid wallflower waiting to bloom.
They can tell I'm dangerous.
Let's go, miss, Hair Care Guy says,
and I hold up my hand
to say *just one second,*
and then I turn
and barf all over the sidewalk.

Good Cop, Bad Cop

In the holding room of Fred Meyer,
they make me pose in front of my stolen goods
like I'm getting my photo taken at Spring Fling,
only instead of being half a couple
posing in front of a cheesy cityscape backdrop,
I have condoms, a clock,
and licorice lined up behind me.

Hair Care Guy thinks this is funny.
Candy and sex—those are my vices too,
he says with a grin.
Ew.
Nice Old Lady doesn't laugh.
That's because she's Bad Cop.
She's not even remorseful, she says,
looking at me.
I realize now might be a good time to act sad,
so I think back to two years ago
after my mom died and my dad had gotten
me a dog for Christmas:
a sheltie from the pound
who was scheduled to die
the next day.

I named him Rufus and slept with him every night
for a month until my father came to tell me

that we were being transferred
to Chicago, and we'd live in an apartment
that didn't allow dogs.

I think back to the day we dropped Rufus off
at a new family's house,
and I think of the look on his face
and his soft ears and his molasses eyes,
and here come the tears
in the back room of the drugstore
as Bad Cop calls my dad
and I bawl in front of all my trinkets,
stupid things you didn't know how much you loved
until they're taken from you
and you can't get them back.

Meditation

I had a hippie science teacher
in the school I went to before this one,
and she told us how she meditated every morning,
and she said when you first learn to do it
you hear all these sounds in the room
you've never heard before
like the air conditioner
or people arguing next door
or a plane above.
It's like you're hyperfocused on everything
because you're trying not to focus on anything.

That's what I'm doing
after my dad picks me up in front of Fred Meyer
and drives me home.
He convinced them not to call the cops
and negotiated for me to go to group therapy instead;
he closed the deal using his expert skills.
I want to say thank you,
but all I can do is
try to breathe
and block out the sound
of his deafening,
disappointed
silence.

SIZE:

PART THREE

5824583647 38824039

"*Guess I'm just another statistic with
another set of clichéd motives.*"

The First Time

The first time I stole,
it was an accident.
I walked out of the store
with a pack of Starburst in my hand
that I'd completely forgotten to pay for.
My mom had
been sick for months already
and she was cranky that day.
I could have gone back but
I felt like I deserved a treat, a present,
something that tastes good,
because if there are forces that decide
to randomly take people away,
there should be forces that decide
to randomly give things for free.

Welcome to Shoplifters Anonymous

A woman with gray flyaway hair announces:
Welcome to Shoplifters Anonymous.
We have some newcomers today,
so bear with me if you've heard this before.
My name is Shawn—
and everyone says, *Hi, Shawn!* so loud
I practically jump out of my seat.
Shawn smiles and proudly says,
I'm a kleptomaniac.
I'm also a codependent and a child of alcoholics,
but that's a different story.
She pauses for laughs,
but there aren't any.
I want to tell all you newcomers
my story from the beginning....

She's just about to start when who walks in—
looking like she wishes she were dead
or, worse, like she stole something
and got caught doing it—
but Tabitha Foster.

TABITHA

ROCK BOTTOM

How the hell did I end up in the basement of Saint Michael's Church on SW Mill in a shit part of town with a boatload of losers? Thank you oh-so-much, Family Friend Jeffrey, for deciding this hellhole is my salvation.

"Make yourself comfortable," says the frizzy-banged woman standing in front of the room. "I'm Shawn. And you are?"

Great. AA has already started.

"Tabitha," I mutter, and flop down in the back, trying to be as invisible as possible. There are some tables, and frayed, grubby brown carpet, and a few dozen women in their thirties and forties, plus one really old man. I didn't think there was going to be anyone my own age, but a few seats over, there's a girl with purple combat boots and a cherry-red dye job that was clearly not achieved with professional input.

Shawn calls her "Maureen," and the girl looks up. "Moe. *Remember?*"

She's got something in Sharpie written on her arm. It's probably a reminder to do drugs or beat somebody up.

The other girl my age is sitting near the front. When Shawn asks her to introduce herself, she says, "I'm Elodie," and when she turns her head, I see her little ski-jump nose and her wavy brown hair, and I realize it's the girl who spilled daiquiri all over me at Derek's party. What are the fucking odds of that? When she bends over to get something out of her purse, I see a camera peeking out of her messenger bag. *That*'s where I've seen her. She's on the yearbook staff. A few months ago, she took a picture of me and Brady. He made some comment to her about how his photo should be on every page.

"Can you pull some strings and make that happen?" he had asked her. Based on the blushing she was doing that day, she's clearly one of dozens of girls at LO High who dream about being his girlfriend. Who wouldn't? He's hot. He's tall. He's practically famous. Lucky me. Now I get to sit here behind one of his superfans. Meanwhile, there's a creepy homeless guy waiting outside so he can blather at me when I leave about how I look Scandinavian. Just when you think you've hit rock bottom, it goes and gets a little bit lower.

*MOE

MARCH 16

Once I saw my fifth-grade teacher Miss Dobson buying douche at the supermarket. She saw me, I saw her, we made eye contact, and I tried to act like I didn't see her vaginal supplies. Still, the shock of seeing her getting her Summer's Eve on was nothing compared to the shock of seeing Tabitha Foster and some goody-two-shoes–looking girl from LO in Shoplifters Anonymous today. I don't know about Goody Two-Shoes, but Tabitha Foster pretty much has everything: money, friends, popularity, a hot boyfriend who worships her. Why would *she* need to steal?

Until now the most interesting person in the class has been Gina, the world's unhappiest housewife, who loves to share her personal details. She has three kids, and her husband works all the time and probably cheats on her at night. I would steal stuff if I were her too. Today she talked about how she's obsessed with stealing panty hose. She said she has more L'eggs panty hose than she'll ever need, but she can't stop—having all of those options makes her feel better. I wrote "L'eggs" on my hand in Sharpie. And then "Panties." That's how bored I was. Although now I'm kind of pumped to hear about the shit Tabitha Foster steals. I hope she unloads all her personal details the way Gina does so I can collect them and make fun of her later.

Dynamics

Moe's real name is Maureen Truax.
I know because Rachelle had me photograph
her and her friends last week,
so "all the social dynamics of LO can be represented."
I finally found them under the bleachers getting high
and they told me to "leave us the fuck alone,"
so I did.
I can't believe
I'm in the same room
with her and Tabitha Foster—
two more opposite people the world has never known.
If this isn't all the social dynamics being represented,
I don't know what is.

TABITHA

SHALL WE, PEOPLE?

"The reasons we shoplift are varied, but they're tied together by the euphoria of getting something for free, the same euphoria any addict feels when getting a hit of a drug," Shawn says, waving away a fly that is hungrily circling her frizzy ponytail. "For some of us, shoplifting is motivated by loss. Losing a person, or a job, or income. There's a hole inside, and stealing fills it. For others, stealing is an act of rebellion against a world we can't control."

As she drones on, I look down at the heart with the initials *BW* carved into the wood on the desk, next to *KL* and *MK*. Obviously a lot of people have sat in this desk before I did. Guess I'm just another statistic with another set of clichéd motives. "Some of us steal because it's a justified payback for how much we give to others and how little they give back to us," Shawn continues. "And for some of us, stealing is a relief mechanism for anxiety, frustration, or depression."

A Desperate Housewife raises her hand.

"Yes, Gina?"

"How do you know if you're depressed?"

"Uh, if you live in Hillsboro and have nothing to do but steal panty hose?" Moe offers.

Shawn glares at her, then turns to the Desperate Housewife.

"Depression is quite common, and there are a number of ways to identify it and treat it. We can discuss the symptoms privately, or I can refer you to a psychiatrist, if you'd like."

Gina nods, looking even more depressed.

"Now, back to the topic at hand. Who here knows what percentage of Americans shoplift?" No one raises a hand. "Ten percent. And it's rising every year. So I want to commend all of you in this room for being here and bravely addressing your addiction. Let's stop the increase, shall we, people?" She gives a little fist pump for good measure.

I'm officially trapped in a Lifetime Television Movie for Women.

★MOE

MARCH 20

For some of these goobers, I think SA meetings are a way to complain about life, or attempt to make people feel sorry for them, or get a free cookie on the way out. I myself find some of the stories and lessons amusing. For the first few months, I'm pretty sure Shawn thought I was taking detailed notes to better myself, but I was actually writing down people's dos and don'ts of shoplifting. Like "Don't act guilty" or "Don't steal from people you know" or "Do steal from chain stores" or "If possible, steal cheese." I'm sure these things will all be helpful to me later in life when I grow up and become a sterling member of society and a role model for humans everywhere.

Montagues and Capulets

Ms. Hoberman is obsessed
with the Montagues and the Capulets.
To prepare for our field trip to see *Romeo and Juliet*,
she added the crests of Juliet's family
and Romeo's family to the never-ending flood
of Shakespeare-themed trinkets on her desk.
Kids make fun of her obsession with Shakespeare
the way my mom's students
probably made fun of her obsession with movies
back when she taught Cinema Studies.
She made me watch old black-and-white ones
with people saying sparkling things and dancing
and doing what she called a "meet cute."
It's where the characters
first meet in some endearing, unexpected way:

a hitchhike or a car crash,
a blind date or a job interview.
Although in my case,
I guess, when you spill a drink on Tabitha Foster
and she yells at you afterward,
it's really more of a "meet ugly."

TABITHA

THE MEMOIR I DON'T WRITE

I'm doodling on my notebook in third-period Creative Writing in an attempt to avoid making eye contact with anyone. Miraculously, I've managed to steer clear of long conversations with people since Derek's party five days ago. However, I feel Jason Baines smirking at me from a few chairs over. This is one of those moments I wish life were a *Final Destination* movie and a random chain saw would fly from the hand of a gardener outside and smash through an open window to violently saw Jason Baines in half.

Distracting me from my fantasy of carnage is Ms. Hoberman, saying, "Your parents need to sign your *Romeo and Juliet* field-trip forms by Wednesday."

Serena Bell is staring at me and whispering something to Kacey Madigan. I look back down at my doodles, which consist of a heart with a knife in it and a monkey face. Clearly, I have no artistic ability.

"For today's free-write, I want you to write a short memoir about your family," Ms. Hoberman continues. "It can be in poetry or prose, comedic or dramatic—obviously it doesn't have to be as dramatic as the Montagues and the Capulets, but I'd love for you to be creative and candid."

Writing about my family with candor or creativity doesn't sound fun. What's there to say? My dad hooks up with women who aren't my mom? Or once I saw him on a date with a brunette at Le Bouchon downtown as they sat in front of candles and ate snails on plates? Should I write that he was saying something that made her laugh? Because for an expert at making people miserable, my dad's actually a pretty funny guy?

Frankly, I'd rather get an incomplete than say any of that. I don't need to dredge up any more reminders of my dad; I already get those a few times a week when I catch a glimpse of his briefcase in the front hall, sitting there like a fantasy of hello and a promise of good-bye.

LUNCH

I wish I could say our cafeteria wasn't like a teen movie where there's a whole by-the-numbers social structure and the dorks sit here and the pretty people sit there and the theater people sit over there and the lax bros sit there and who knows who else sits who knows where else, but it pretty much *is* that way.

"This corn dog is disgusting," says Kayla as she tries to bite into the soggy, khaki-colored tube.

I gag at the sight of it. "I don't know why you eat that crap," I say, opening my carrots and hummus.

"I like pizza day," Kayla says. "When *is* pizza day?"

Patrick Cushman walks by. "I got the recipe from the lunch lady. If you ever want to try to make it at home."

"You can do that?" Kayla says.

"That's weird. Who knows how to make pizza?" Taryn finally looks up, flicking a crouton crumb off the sleeve of her tight red shirt. Her boobs look like they're going to fall out of it. Sometimes I wish this school had a dress code.

"Apparently, he does," I say, with a glance at Patrick.

Patrick smiles. "Well, I wouldn't recommend it. It's not the same without that special LO grease pool on top." He walks on, heading over to sit with the theater geeks. At least I think they're theater geeks. One of them is doing some kind of loud imitation of Will Smith from *Independence Day*. Patrick seems to find it amusing. I want to tell him not to encourage stupidity, because it only creates more of it. Instead, I get beaned in the head with a French fry.

I look up to see Brady standing there.

"Wanna french?" he asks, grinning at me. He sits down at the far end of the table and reaches over to grab another of Jason's fries off his plate.

"Hey, dude, that was mine!" Jason cries, protectively covering them. "You can't be throwing my fries around!"

For the past two days, I've been avoiding Brady and succeeding because he had extra lacrosse practice and meetings during lunch hour and a big game last night. They won, so now he's full of bravado.

"Uh, no." I choose to ignore him and turn my attention back to Kayla, who's dissecting her corn dog like a mortician in the middle of an autopsy.

"What is the 'dog' in the 'corn' made of?" Kayla wrinkles her nose at it.

"Don't try to understand it," I respond. "It will only cause you pain."

Taryn looks over at Brady. "You guys were uh-mazing last night," she simpers. I look at her sharply. Seriously? She's going to gush over his athletic prowess? Girl code is clearly dead.

"I missed my good-luck charm, but I guess I'm so awesome I don't need it." He nods pointedly to me. I pretend my hummus is the most interesting thing in the world. It has red peppers in it. And cumin. And some other sort of spice that tastes like—

"Can I come sit with you so you can congratulate me

and we can talk about the sexy dress you're going to wear to the Spring Fling?" Brady says. He's enjoying having an audience of Jason and his friends and all the other people at our table. Taryn elbows me, and I sigh. Sometimes it's just easier to let things go back to normal than it is to try to change them.

"Sure." I shrug.

Brady stands up and walks over, plunking his tray down across from me. On it is a Diet Coke and a huge salad with vinaigrette dressing. He doesn't eat cheese or carbs or drink regular Coke ever. He's like a girl that way.

"Hi, Tabs," he says softly. I finally look up. He's wearing a blue shirt that makes his eyes look like the sky on a perfect summer day.

"Miss me?" he asks. Fuck. He's got such a cute smile.

"Miss *me*?" I retort.

"Like crazy," he says, and then pelts a pickle at me. I hurl one back at him. Then Kayla throws one at Jason, and Taryn flings a splot of hummus at some poor nerd sitting at another table, and someone else chucks something else because this is what happens when you start something that looks like so much fun. Everyone else joins in because they're afraid of what they'll miss out on if they don't.

MOE

MARCH 28

My aunt keeps bugging me to invite friends over to hang out at the house. I don't know why she's so into it. The last time I had Alex and Janet over, we spilled L'Oreal Superior Preference Intense Dark Red hair dye on the floor while Alex was coloring my hair and Aunt B was super pissed. And she hasn't forgotten about it because every time she passes the spot on the floor she mutters, "Damn hair dye." I try not to make her mad, but I always seem to anyway. At least my hair turned out okay. Although I can't say as much about that big red stain on the living room rug.

Her insisting I have friends over probably means Marc's been telling her he doesn't like my friends or they're not good for me, so she's worried I'm on drugs or something and wants to keep tabs on me. I find it kind of entertaining, so I constantly itch my nose when she's around. Yesterday I even left a rolled-up dollar bill on the kitchen counter with powdered sugar on it. She called me a wiseass. I want to tell her to lighten up, but it doesn't take a genius to notice when you tell people that, it usually has the opposite effect and they get hostile. I wish she had more of a sense of humor, just like she probably wishes I had a totally different personality.

TABITHA

YOU BET

"Want to come over and watch *Top Model*?" Taryn asks me in sixth period. She loves reality TV. She's Generation Kardashian all the way. I guess you've got to admire them for cashing in on their tits, ass, and a desperate need for attention, but it seems like there has to be more to life than fragrance lines and endorsement deals. I don't feel guilty for hoisting a fragrance or two by Khloe or Kim or jeggings by Kristin Cavallari; they've all stolen hours of my life at Taryn's behest.

Not today, though. Today I have to pay penance for my sins at Shoplifters Anonymous. I lie and tell Taryn I'm doing an SAT prep course across town.

"Yuck. I'm sorry," she says, and doesn't press for more details. As predicted.

When my mom drops me off, I steal her lemon-lime

vitaminwater and ask her to e-mail Jeffrey and see if it's possible for me to get through the class in less than the normal required time.

"Why do you ask?" she says.

"Because it sucks, and there're people from my school in there I don't want to deal with."

"Okay," she says. "But in the meantime, why don't you try to make the best of it?"

That means she won't be e-mailing Jeffrey.

I get out of the car and slink into the building, past the AA meeting, the Al-Anon meeting, the Nicotine Anonymous meeting, down into the basement, and into a chair in the back row. I immediately bury myself in Facebook on my phone.

"Afternoon, lovelies!"

I'm drop-kicked out of my status-update reverie by Shawn's chipper voice.

"Tabitha, can you please turn off your phone?"

I obey as she launches into a "Group Participation and Identification Exercise." As if to underscore the humiliation, she pairs me with Moe and Elodie. We drag our chairs together awkwardly as Shawn adds, "And, Harold, why don't you join them too?" A guy who looks like he's ninety-five years old slowly stands and starts to drag his chair over.

Shawn calls out, "Moe, can you help Harold?"

Moe takes Harold's chair from him and hoists it over her head, then drops it down, practically smashing it on my foot. I shoot her a dirty look. She doesn't seem to notice.

"I want you to go around with your group-mates," Shawn says, "and share exactly why you're here and what regrets you have about getting caught."

I keep my head down and curse myself for ever being stupid enough to look at the blog with Alexa Chung wearing that Maya Brenner bracelet.

Moe clears her throat. "My regret is that I shouldn't have broken into someone's car and stolen their CDs," she says with a shrug. "I don't even have a CD player." Then she looks at Elodie. "What'd you take?"

"Stuff from Fred Meyer," Elodie says quietly.

"Like what?"

"I don't know...licorice, a clock, condoms—"

"Condoms?" I practically snarf my vitaminwater.

Moe laughs. "Awesome."

"I may need them," Elodie says, defensive.

"Why'd you steal condoms?" I ask, genuinely curious. This girl doesn't exactly radiate sexual activity.

"She probably stole them to have sex," Moe says. "Duh."

"With who?" I volley back. Obviously, she's never stolen condoms. It's not that she looks like a total square, but girls who've had sex look different from those who haven't. Not to say that I've had a ton of it and I'm some kind of expert. But I've had enough to at least know what I'm missing and what I'm not missing.

"Do you have a boyfriend?" I press.

"Oh, so a committed relationship is required to bone somebody?" Moe asks.

Harold snorts, and we look over. He's sound asleep in his chair. I guess conversations about illegally acquired birth control don't really interest him.

"What about *you*?" Elodie says, pissy. "What did you take?"

Crap. This is exactly what I wanted to avoid. Complete strangers knowing my business. But you know what? At least I was taking something more exciting than condoms that would only turn to dust in my purse.

"Designer bracelet." I shrug, nonchalant.

"Why would you need to steal something? Aren't you rich?" Moe asks.

"It's none of your business," I fire back.

Moe looks at Elodie. "She probably just forgot to lay down her daddy's black AmEx. Either that or she's claiming she stole something expensive so she can sound like a badass."

Elodie and Moe exchange a smile, like they're laughing at me.

"Fine," I say. "Let's prove it, then."

Moe laughs. "What the hell are you talking about?"

"Just what I said." I glare at her.

Elodie looks back and forth between us.

"After class we go lift the best stuff we can," I continue. "Then we meet afterward at Pizzicato and compare notes."

Harold snorts again. This time it's so violent he's woken himself up.

"Where am I?" he asks, genuinely confused.

"You're in Shoplifters Anonymous with a bunch of girls who are about to have some fun," Moe says, then glances at me. "Your friends hang out at Pizzicato, so we should probably meet at the Roxy instead."

She has a point.

"Fine," I say. "The Roxy it is."

Elodie looks at us. "I'm in."

"You're into what?" Shawn asks, passing by our table right at that exact moment.

"Identifying with each other. Right, guys?" Moe smirks at us.

"Right," I add.

"Indeedy," Harold says, proud to be included.

"Excellent," Shawn says, and walks off, pleased with our personal growth and utterly oblivious as to what was about to happen.

Powell's

I weave through the literary mecca
that is Powell's,
a place so big it must employ half of P-town.
It's famous for not letting lifters get away
with anything bigger than a paper clip,
but I'm up for the challenge.
I tuck *The Collected Poems of Emily Dickinson*
and *Broken Soup* by Jenny Valentine
underneath a copy of *The Merc*
and I pay for a lone hummingbird bookmark
and smile sweetly
at the girl at the counter
and I walk through the sensors,
which don't go off,
since I removed all the magnetic strips from the books—

but then I stop.
Shit.
If this is a war
about who's the biggest badass,
a girl who stole two books
isn't exactly
going to win.

TABITHA

THE ROXY

I'm sitting in a leopard-print chair five feet away from a ginormous crucified Jesus. His feet dangle above a jukebox.

"Sweet Jesus," I crack. The shiny Pepto-pink walls are starting to make me loopy.

"I like how his crown of thorns is made of lights," Elodie says, taking a bite of her Quentin Tarantuna, which is basically a tuna melt on rye with a ridiculous name. We share a Lord of the Fries, dripping in chili cheese. Calories don't count if you've been shoplifting.

After she takes a big slurp of Dr Pepper, Moe points and asks me if I know anyone here.

"Like who?" I say. The only people here are a Mohawked guy and a smattering of scrawny hipster twentysomethings sitting in the corner.

She shrugs. "I just wanted to be sure you were saved the embarrassment of being affiliated with us."

"I never said I was embarrassed," I snap.

"But aren't you?" Elodie asks, curious.

"She obviously is." Moe crams a fry into her mouth, then turns to me.

Whatever. Now I just want to win this infuriatingly dumb idea for a contest and leave. I yank out a kelly-green Betsey Johnson shirt and a strappy minidress. "Betsey Johnson. Admire and weep."

Elodie fingers the dress with an impressed murmur. Moe reaches down and pulls out her bag, dumping a bunch of stuff all over the table.

Elodie inhales sharply. "Whoa."

Moe holds up a bunch of cherry-flavored condoms. "Licorice, anyone?"

Elodie shoots her a look, and Moe shrugs. "I may need them to have *actual* sex."

I hold up a pair of fuzzy pink handcuffs and raise an eyebrow.

"Those are for you," Moe says to me. "You wear pink, right?"

"I do." I smirk. "Thanks."

Elodie asks, "Where did you get all this stuff?"

Moe shrugs. "Spartacus."

"You went into *Spartacus*?" I have to admit, I'm impressed. And a little ooked out. It's a sex shop crawling with leather daddies and porn lovers. One time Brady dared me to go in there, but I couldn't do it. Too much perv DNA on the premises.

"If you got caught there, they'd probably sell you into sex slavery," I say with a sniff.

"I'm the last person they'd want to bust. They were too busy trying to stop a guy from putting his penis inside a blow-up doll."

"Ew." Elodie looks traumatized.

"Where did *you* go?" I ask Elodie.

She looks embarrassed, then reaches to the seat next to her, pulling her overcoat onto the table and taking a novel and a book of poems out of the pockets.

I pick up *The Collected Poems of Emily Dickinson.* "Didn't Ms. Hoberman assign us this a few months ago?"

Elodie nods. Then she pulls out a perfect little clutch. It's chic and black, with a cute gold buckle. "I also went to Coach," she says modestly.

"That's, like, four hundred bucks!" I gasp. I can't help it.

"I knew this girl was trouble," Moe says.

"How'd you pull that off?" I ask.

She shrugs. "It's a perk of being a good girl. No one suspects you'll ever do anything bad."

As I stare at her, jaw dropped, Moe suddenly blurts out, "Oh, fuck."

We turn to see what Moe's looking at: a tall, pockmarked guy with wispy hair and a really creepy grimace on his face. Even though he's skinny, he's muscular and strong-looking.

"It's the blow-up doll guy!" Moe whispers.

"That's him?" I'm actually kind of scared.

"Don't look at him!" Moe hisses, and we whip back around.

"He tried to get me to go in the back of the store with him," she says, looking freaked out. "He told me if I didn't, he'd call the cops and tell them I was stealing."

Elodie panics. "What?!"

"He's coming over here!" Moe says. Elodie panics, grabbing my arm.

"Should we scream?" I'm actually worried I may lose my shit.

From Moe's eyes, I can tell he's about to appear right over my shoulder. "Oh God!" she yells.

We gasp and spin around—only to see a little girl standing behind us.

Elodie deflates, trying to catch her breath. Moe keels over with laughter.

"You asshole!" I say.

Moe points. "Looks like he's getting himself some pie." The skinny guy is sitting in a booth, placing an order with the waitress and looking utterly benign.

Moe starts laughing so hard she drops half her sandwich on her lap.

"You've got Tarantuna on your pants," Elodie says, pointing.

"So he didn't really say that to you in the sex shop?" I can't believe she would make up that shit.

"Hell, no," she says. "I've never even seen that dude before."

"What?" I can't believe she tricked us like that.

"And there was no blow-up doll," Moe adds. "Well, it wasn't inflated, anyway. But it was a pretty good story, right?"

I punch her in the arm, knocking over my milk shake and making a gross, disgusting mess, but I have to say that even though I want to kill her, I'm pretty sure I haven't laughed this hard in six months.

Buried Treasure

Last week they had a story on the news
about a stolen sculpture
worth sixty million dollars
that the police found buried in a box
in the forest.
The thief had put it in the ground years earlier
for safekeeping
until finally he got so scared about being caught
he decided to turn himself in.
He led the authorities out into the woods
and watched
as they dug up his prize.

I relay this to Tabitha and Moe
as we walk down Stark Street, haul in hand,

and we agree
that maybe the thief felt proud
when they pulled the statue out;
he'd finally gotten to tell someone
what he'd accomplished,
he'd finally gotten to confess his crime
in all its glorious detail,
he'd finally realized that stealing in solitude
can drive you crazy,
the loneliness of a victory can overtake you
and maybe the only thing
that makes it worthwhile
is having someone to share it with.

★MOE

APRIL 8

Elodie was surprised when I told her I'd already read *Broken Soup*. Tabitha said she hadn't read it, so Elodie gave her the copy. Hanging out at the Roxy with them was more fun than listening to Alex lay out a plan to TP some nerd's house, but it wasn't like we were super buddy-buddy or anything. Obviously, I didn't tell them about Noah or even that I like to read while taking a bath. It's none of their business. I guess if they were judging a book by the cover, mine would be different from what's on the inside too.

TABITHA

VAPORS

It's one of those rare Portland spring nights when it's not too cold, so I roll down the windows on the drive home. I think of Elodie pulling out that little Coach clutch and how fun it was to sprint down the street in a pack, like we were on the run, like we were real criminals.

I stop at a light and glance over at the car next to me. The guy driving it smiles at me. He looks like a pimp. He probably *is* a pimp. I once read that Portland has more pimps and strip clubs per capita than other places, but then again, I've never spent much time anywhere else, so how would I know if that's accurate?

I give him a small smile back. I might as well. It's not like a pimp is going to follow me home and get me to marry him. Then again, maybe he would. I'm relieved when he turns off onto a side street. I drive on through

Southshore, the pines pointing into the dark sky, reminding all who pass that even if you're rooted into the ground, the only place you can really grow is up.

Later that night, when my mom's key turns in the lock, I head into the kitchen to meet her.

"How was your night?" I ask when she comes in. Her eyeliner is all smudgy and flaky.

"Oh, it was lovely, honey," she says, opening a vitaminwater and popping some vitamin B12. It's her favorite hangover cure that doesn't cure much, but she still swears by it. She throws in a multivitamin, and Lord knows whatever minerals and antiaging pills for good measure, and chugs them all down. "How was your group therapy?"

I shrug. "It's not really therapy, but whatever."

"So you're not going to shoplift again, right?"

"Do I look like an idiot?" I sneer, even though I hate lying to her, especially when she looks all disheveled and sort of lonely standing there.

"You don't need to be so hard on me." She starts getting teary.

"I'm not!" I say, then I decide, *What the heck*, and I reach out and hug her good night. Her fingers linger on my back for a second, like a vapor drifting above warm liquor that's just been poured into a frosty glass.

"See you in the morning," I say. Misty-eyed, my mom nods and smiles at me, making me wish that I'd left the room sooner or left out the whole hugging part, but what can you do? Sometimes it's nice to be nice.

Coq au Vin

Tonight at dinner, my father asks me
how the program is going.
I take a bite of Jenna's coq au vin
that she made from her French
   cooking class recipe,
which is weird because she can barely make a salad,
so how is she learning to make French food?
He asks me if I thought shoplifting was worth
the disappointment and embarrassment
and I chew and chew
the same piece of chicken
and he says he doesn't know why
I would steal
when he works hard so I can afford
whatever I need or want

and then Jenna interrupts to ask
if anyone would like some more *poulet*
and even though I can barely swallow
the bite of never-ending drumstick
I've been chewing and chewing
I say, *Yes, please*,
and for once, my stepmom's food
tastes like salvation.

APRIL 9

Seeing Noah flirting with Kayla Lee in the parking lot doesn't upset me as much as you'd think it would. I walked right past him. I know he saw me, and I'm sure he was wondering where I was going. I like that he doesn't know what I do after school. He just keeps sending me texts asking me where I go. So far his guesses are:

1. in training for a beauty pageant (ha-ha, he knows I think Miss America is the most evil thing ever)
2. singing lessons
3. needlepoint class

Today he sent me one that said, ARE YOU A SPY? And I wrote back, YOU'LL NEVER KNOW.

TABITHA

FLOWER

When Brady sees me in the hallway before lunch, he doesn't look happy. We hooked up a few days ago after school, but I kept the conversation to a minimum. When he calls, I mostly send his calls to voice mail, but it's pretty hard to avoid all contact if your locker is right next to his, and your friends are his friends. It takes timing and coordination, like being a thief.

He catches up to me as I'm walking to the snack bar. "Hey."

"Hey." I smile, but it feels like a grimace.

Brady glares at me. "What's your problem?"

"What do you mean?" I shrug, playing as innocent as possible, even though I feel as guilty as possible.

"You've been acting all hot and cold for, like, a month.... What the hell? Why are you being a freak?"

I can't help but laugh. I sometimes laugh when I get nervous. I guess it's a bad sign when your boyfriend makes you nervous.

"And now you're laughing at me?!" He looks piiiissed.

"No!" I say, but then another little laugh comes out. I must sound like a person on the brink of hysteria. Brady steps closer and grabs my arm, pinching it. Hard.

"Ow!" I cry, yanking away. I wince and look down. A little red mark flowers on my triceps.

"Whatever," he says. Then turns and walks away.

I watch him go, and wonder if a normal girl would have pinched him back. Or screamed. But what's the point of that? I'd be making yet another scene.

I stand there a second before turning and robotically walking toward the snack bar as the spot on my arm blossoms into something less than beautiful.

FUN

Even after I buy my veggie dip and crackers, I still can't stop shaking. I head for the library so I can eat my lunch somewhere away from everyone. I keep telling myself, *This is what happens in relationships—people accidentally hurt each other. It's a common occurrence.*

I walk past Keith Savage and Zoe Amato leaning against the lockers. Zoe wipes her eyes, and I can tell she's been crying but she's pretending she hasn't. At first I think it's just another fighting couple and it makes me sick, until I see how Keith is staring at her, and he reaches up to touch her shoulder. It's gentle, like he's going to apologize for saying or doing something wrong—proving, I guess, that even if people fight, they're still capable of loving each other. That kind of love makes me want to cry, so I keep walking.

I pass all the Spring Fling signs that promise FUN FUN FUN!!! They only stress me out more. The last time I kissed Brady by the lockers and actually enjoyed it was over four weeks ago, and he'd asked me what color dress I was wearing to the Fling. But there's no reason to think of that now, because giving it airspace in my head just makes the pit in my stomach bigger.

I throw my veggie dip and crackers in the trash and decide to go to Ms. Hoberman's class early. As I'm heading into her room, I pass Moe walking out. She must have fourth period with her or something. She's with a few burnouts who are being kind of loud.

"What the hell's a villanelle?" a pimply guy with a faux-hawk says. "Is that some kind of zombie pill?"

The other girl with bleach-blond hair and a nose ring laughs. "I want zombie pills. Like, now." I think her name is Alex. I remember because last year she got accused of setting Taryn's backpack on fire. Not like a full blaze or anything, but enough to cause the principal to ban all lighters and matches on school grounds.

As Moe passes we meet eyes for a second, and then she gives me a wink. None of her friends seem to notice. She keeps walking one way, me the other. Weirdly, it's the only thing that gets me a little bit closer to feeling better.

SIZE:

PART
FOUR

5824583647 38824039

*"Maybe we will save the world
one trinket at a time."*

Gossip

On the bus ride downtown,
I sit next to Rachelle, who's gossiping
about what girl blew which guy
and which football player's dick is bigger
and who's hooking up and who's breaking up,
because she says it's her job as an editor
to know everybody's dirty secrets.

She leaves to walk
to the back of the bus
to get a quote from Samantha about the
Shakespeare trip
for the "Outings & Aboutings" page.
Sometimes I think she uses Yearbook as an excuse
to talk to kids who wouldn't

give her the time of day before.
In a way I don't blame her;
we're all on a quest to be noticed—
except maybe Moe,
who's fully snoring six seats in front of me.

When Rachelle comes back,
she's amped up because
Samantha introduced her to Tabitha Foster,
"who was a total bitch."
She's not a bitch, I say without thinking,
and Rachelle says, *How do you know?*
and I cover and say, *I have a class with her.*
She asks what class.
If I were a gossip I'd say,
A class for people who steal,
and Rachelle would die of happiness
because it's a dirty secret no one knows.
But I just shrug and say, *Geometry Two*, and Rachelle says,
Well, trust me, she's a bitch,
and I say, *You're probably right*,
because I realize that with Rachelle,
if you don't have anything mean to say,
she doesn't want to hear anything at all.

TABITHA

NOBODY

I find my seat in the theater next to Taryn, who's buried in her phone.

"Who're you texting?" I ask, glancing over her shoulder.

She yanks the screen away. "Nobody," she says.

I shoot daggers at her. I'm not sure when she got the idea that she could talk to me like that.

There are about sixty LO kids here in the theater, mixed with a few hundred people my parents' age. The room has little balconies and berry-red seats and gold walls. A few of the people smiled at us as we came in, like they approved of what culturally advanced students we were.

I straighten my dress, a Nanette Lepore I stole from Souchi a few months ago when I was shopping with my mom. It was risky to steal it when she was standing ten feet away from me, but that was half the fun of it. Besides, she wasn't exactly fully aware of her surroundings.

I peer up at the little balconies before spotting Elodie, sitting four rows in front of us. She's with another girl from Yearbook, snapping pictures of the old baroque theater with her camera. Moe is sitting right in front of me. If I squint hard enough, I can almost read what she's writing in her notebook…which she probably wouldn't appreciate. Although she'd be more chill about it than Taryn was when I tried to read her phone. She was a dick. But I guess no matter what, Taryn and I have a history together. For what it's worth.

As the lights dim, Ms. Hoberman looks rapt. The parental-age people in their suits and dresses start to clap. I sink down in my seat as the red curtain rises up and away. I can't help feeling like whatever's going to happen isn't going to be good. I've read the play, and everybody knows this is a tragedy.

*MOE

APRIL 15

Why do we have to read a play and then sit through a shitty performance of it? I feel bad for those suckers onstage because this is going to be the highlight of their acting careers. Fortunately I can write observations in here of how I definitely smelled a fart in the lobby and now I'm pretty sure Mercutio has a boner. Can you imagine getting a chubby onstage? I'd play it off like I didn't care, but inside I'd be mortified. There are tons of annoying things about being a girl, but at least we don't have to deal with phantom boners. I wrote a note on a piece of paper and covertly flashed it to Tabitha, but I don't think she got the joke. I wrote, "Mercutio's giving the full salute." She looked confused. Once I explain it, I'm sure she'll think it's funny. Or maybe she'll be annoyed I tried to flash her a note in public, but who cares. Somebody needed to appreciate my humor, and it might as well be her.

Blush

After the play is over, Ms. Hoberman gathers everyone—
but Keith Savage and Zoe Amato, who are off making
   out,
and Heather Rardin and Oliver Montone, who are
   probably
doing more than that in an alley somewhere—
and gives a virtual soliloquy
about the themes of the play,
like fate versus free will and the power of love
and the passage of time
and the individual versus society,
and how society and your family
want you to behave one way
even if your heart tells you
to act differently.

*　　*　　*

Then she gets her program
signed by all the actors
and she blushes when the guy who played Mercutio
puts his arm around her for a photo,
and when Patrick Cushman tries to look at her program
she slaps his hand away.
She says she needs to get it laminated
and then we can look at it.
Clearly this is her new prized possession
of all prized possessions.

As I take a picture for the yearbook,
Moe makes a peace sign over Patrick's head
and I try not to laugh.
I guess if there ever was an individual against society,
it would probably be her.

TABITHA

MODERATELY APPEALING

On the bus home, Patrick Cushman passes out gum. When he asks me if I want any, I decline. Gum is a disappointment. It seems like the flavor never lasts more than a minute. It always leaves you wanting more.

"He's just trying to impress you," Taryn says, glaring over at Patrick. "Because he said he stole it from 7-Eleven."

"He stole it?" I ask. This is a surprise.

"Apparently." Taryn rolls her eyes. "Only idiots would shoplift," she sneers.

I'm glad I never confided my extracurricular activities to her. Once when I was drunk, I was tempted to tell Kayla, but then she started telling a long story about hooking up with some hippie guy she met from Lewis & Clark and how she was totally scared he gave her herpes. Hence, the moment passed, and I didn't bring it up again.

Now girls I wasn't aware of three weeks ago know more stuff about me than some of my friends do. When Moe tried to get my attention tonight, at first I was irritated. Then the whole rest of the play I kept intermittently wishing I could figure out what the hell she'd written. I bet it was funny.

Patrick Cushman leans over to me. "It's watermelon. You sure you don't want a piece?"

"Fine," I say, reluctantly taking one. He grins and I ask, "So, was it worth the risk?"

He looks a little surprised by the question. "To be honest, I've never stolen anything in my life. It was a complete accident that I'm reframing as a criminal act in order to make myself sound impressive."

I smile. He's kind of cute, actually. Lanky limbs. Green eyes with a little bit of a sparkle. He's not as buff as Brady, but he has nice hands. I get a sudden flash of him putting my sweatshirt around my shoulders that day as we left the nurse's office after my dodgeball debacle. He may have been creeping on me, but it was in the most gentlemanly way possible.

"I'm not sure if 'impressive' applies. Maybe 'moderately appealing'?"

He laughs. "I'll take that."

I unwrap the piece of gum he hands me and put it in my mouth. "*Mmm.* Definitely worth it."

"Here," he says. "Keep one for the road. It always loses its flavor too quick."

He walks back to join his friends, and I watch him go. Taryn is staring over at me like *WTF?* so I just put on my iPod and concentrate on making the taste of watermelon last as long as it possibly can.

*MOE

APRIL 16

Aunt B was working the night shift at the hospital, so Marc was waiting up for me after I got home from the play.

As far as brothers go, he's not bad, aside from the time when I was seven and he got us lost on that "secret" ski run only he knew about at Mount Hood Meadows. It was right before our parents had their accident. Ski patrol had to go out looking for us. When we finally made it back to the lodge, our parents were pissed, because tons of people die up there. Usually hikers, but still. They even made us stay in the cabin all weekend, and our mom wouldn't let us get hot chocolate. I loved hot chocolate, so I stopped talking to Marc for a week, until he used all of his allowance money to buy me three boxes of

Nestlé cocoa with little mini marshmallows and I for-
gave him.

I didn't really have much to report about the play, but Marc
didn't care. He just likes to know I'm home before he goes
to sleep.

TABITHA

CRACK

When Moe walks into Shoplifters Anonymous, she stops at my chair. "Meet up after?" she asks me. I nod, and she says, "Cool. I'll tell Elodie."

We sit there for an hour and forty minutes as Shawn shows an ancient educational film about the perils of shoplifting. It features Winona Ryder doing community service and talking about how wrong it is to steal. She's wearing a cute vintage dress and tiny diamond studs. She doesn't seem super regretful even though all she talks about is how sorry she is. You'd think as an actress, she'd want to act a little more apologetic, but then again, if somebody made me do a video after I got caught shoplifting, I'd probably be insanely annoyed.

After the movie, Shawn makes one of her efforts to lead a productive discussion.

"We spoke about 'relief mechanisms,' right? Well, the problem with alleviating your issue with kleptomania is that then it just needs to be activated again and again. So you have to sort out what's *causing* your behavior in order to not *need* the behavior."

Why does everything Shawn says sound like Latin? I wish it didn't, because maybe I'd learn something.

"Yes, Gina?"

"I started smoking. Do you think that's a good relief mechanism?" Gina asks.

"I need a relief mechanism to get me away from Gina," Moe whispers.

I try not to laugh, because Gina kind of reminds me of my mom in some weird way. Failed hopes and dreams and all that.

"Okay, well, you have to be careful to not replace one addiction with another, but if you keep working on yourself and being honest about your issues, then you're already heading in the right direction," Shawn says. I've got to hand it to her: The woman can attempt to turn any inquiry into a Positive Learning Experience.

After class, I meet Elodie and Moe at the Pepsi machine in the hall.

"Dude, Gina's gonna end up on crack before this is over," Moe says.

"You think?" Elodie asks, worried.

"What else is there for her to do?" Moe says, taking a big swig of her soda, then makes a face and holds the bottle up to the light. "Does anyone else think Mountain Dew is poisonous? I mean, it looks like cat pee."

"Maybe you should give some to Gina," Elodie offers just as Shawn walks up.

"Hey, girls," she says, all smiles.

We all kind of mutter hello, and she says, "I think it's great you guys are forming support for one another. It's a really important part of the work."

"Super," Moe says, a placid smile on her face. Elodie looks like she's about to start laughing. Shawn frowns. The last thing in the world I want is to have to take this whole program over again just because of Moe, so I blurt, "I had to deal with my dad's addiction for a while, so I agree about the whole support-system thing."

"Really?" Shawn goes from frowny to intrigued.

I nod. "Definitely."

"Well, thank you for sharing that." She touches my elbow with compassion, looking pleased with this breakthrough. She gives us all a supportive nod and walks off down the hall, the fringe on her beaded vest jangling jauntily.

Elodie looks at me, curious.

"What's your dad addicted to?"

I think for a second. "Uh, vaginas?"

"You can't be addicted to that," Elodie says. "Can you?"

"Dude, they have, like, Love and Sex Addicts Anonymous down the hall," Moe says. "So obviously you can."

"I'm pretty sure he's in Screw Whoever He Wants All the Time Anonymous," I say.

"So your parents are divorced?" Elodie asks.

"Nope. Happily married, according to my mom."

"She doesn't know he cheats?" Moe says.

"Sure she does. She just doesn't like to admit it to herself."

The girls stare at me for a second, and finally Moe observes, "No wonder you're so fucked up."

I want to tell her to shut up, but it feels good to come clean about everything. Secrets have more power if they're buried in a box, so it can be good to dig them up and take them out into the open.

"You guys want to come over to my house?" Moe asks. She looks at me. "My aunt says I should invite people over more often. Obviously, she thinks I'm as fucked up as you are."

Spies Like Us

On our way out of class,
Moe joked maybe we are being
secretly recruited by the CIA,
and maybe Shawn is a top agent
sent to find new trainees,
and we are the chosen ones.
Maybe we will learn to carry state secrets
and smuggle microchips
and seduce bad guys.
Maybe we will save the world
one trinket
at a time.

TABITHA

THE ASSIGNMENT

"So, did you have fun at *Romeo and Juliet*?" Elodie asks us. We're walking downtown past Pioneer Courthouse Square, where all kinds of people are basking in the almost sunny day. Some dude is banging on plastic tubs like they're drums.

"It wasn't so bad," Moe offers. "I hope Ms. H got that guy's number. The erect one. I feel like he could have a positive impact on her life." She makes a hip thrusting motion, and Elodie squeals.

"Did she assign you guys to write some stupid creative memoir about your family? Or was that just our class?" I ask.

"Yeah. Annoying. What's there to say?" Moe shrugs, taking a piece of turkey jerky out of her bag and shoving it into her mouth.

"Trust me, I've got plenty to say about my parents," I say. "I just don't want to say it in an assignment in Ms. Hoberman's class."

"So, have you written it?" Elodie asks us both.

"No. And I don't plan to."

"The only writing I can do is in my journal. When I go to write a paper, it reeks," says Moe.

"I like writing poems," Elodie says.

"Duh. You're a total poetry type," Moe teases, chasing down her jerky with a chug of Red Bull and swishing it around before she adds, "Poems are dorky."

"They are not!" Elodie looks offended. "What do you think all great songs are? Poetry."

"A great song is a great song. A poem is just a poem," Moe retorts.

"I don't know about poems, but I read blogs," I say. "Have you been to the one by that girl in Chicago who's our age?"

"Blogs by teenagers: also stupid," Moe says.

"No, it's good, trust me." I don't know why I am bothering to try to convince a person who is a known vandal about the validity of a well-known website, so I change the subject. "Let's go get some stuff and meet back here."

"In twenty minutes?" Elodie asks.

"That's barely enough time," whines Moe.

"Nut up," Elodie fires back. She's got surprising balls. Then she blushes. "Sorry. Something my dad used to say."

"See you then," I say. Moe sighs and heads off in one direction, and Elodie and I go in another. If only poor Shawn knew that this particular 10 percent of the population definitely wasn't curbing their shoplifting tendencies but instead fanning the flames as much as possible.

Red

All right, let's see what you got,
I say to Tabitha.
We're waiting for Moe back at our meeting spot,
in front of the sculpture of a guy sitting on a bench.
People always freak out because even though he's
   bronze,
they always think he's real.
Tabitha opens her bag
and pulls out a red Prada dress from Mario's.
You should get one of these, she says.
It's not really my style, but I like red.
Red says sexy and mysterious
and dangerous
and everything that I used to not be
but am now totally becoming.

The Sprint

Moe runs up all out of breath: *We gotta go!*
She takes off in a sprint.
Shit! Tabitha says, and we bolt after Moe,
who races out of the square
and around the corner
and up the stairs into a parking garage,
until she drags us behind a Prius
covered in left-wing bumper stickers
like GO GREEN OR GO HOME
and UNFAIRIZONA.
We crouch down, panting,
and after a second Tabitha peeks
around the bumper
and says, *Are they gone?*
Who? Moe says.
Whoever was chasing us, Tabitha says, annoyed.
Oh, that, Moe responds. *I was just seeing how fast you
    guys could run.*
Tabitha looks at her.
Bitch!
Moe grins.
You know you love me.

Screech Crackle Pop

Screech crackle pop.
We are on the light rail going from Pioneer Place
to the Pearl,
a district of swishy shops built on the bones
of abandoned warehouses.
I wish we had a more dignified mode of transport.
Too bad we don't know how to steal cars, Moe says.
She's right.
Hot-wiring is probably far superior
to sitting in plastic seats on the MAX
next to an old guy in a beret
who looks more weirded out by us
than we do by him.

Screech crackle pop.
I snap a shot
of Moe as she turns and looks over her shoulder
flipping me the so-called bird.
I point the camera at Tabitha,
who smiles like a beautiful girl on autopilot.
No smile needed, I say
and she looks confused
so I click the shutter.
Better.

We're almost there, Moe says.
I lean over to Old Beret Guy

and ask, *Can you take a picture of us?*
He takes the camera
and snaps us.
This photo will never be in a yearbook
because who knows what the three of us
even look like together
and it wouldn't make any sense to anyone,
but at least there's proof
this moment existed.

This is us, Moe says at SW Tenth.
I guess she's right:
This is us,
whoever we are.
We scatter off
like birds flying free,
screech crackle pop
all in a flock.

TABITHA

LOSING FEATHERS

At Moe's house, the first thing I notice is the orange-and-blue parrot in the kitchen. The poor thing is missing so many feathers, it's downright bald in spots.

"Does your parrot have alopecia or something?" I ask.

"My aunt says it's because Marc got him high once and he starting picking out his feathers. But I think he was just born with ADD or OCD or something," Moe explains.

"Maybe it's a relief mechanism," Elodie says.

"Thanks, Shawn. Your insight is super profound," Moe says as she heads upstairs, gesturing for us to follow.

Moe's room is surprisingly nice: a queen-size bed with a purple bedspread, and starry wallpaper on the walls, and a few framed photos on the dresser. One of them must be of her parents, who have big smiles on their faces as they stand with two little kids in front of a house. When Elodie asks her, she says, "That's us as little kids. My folks died when I was seven."

"My mom's dead," Elodie says.

"Really?" Moe looks at her, surprised.

"Two years ago. It sucks. My dad got remarried."

"Is your stepmom cool?" Moe asks.

Elodie shrugs. "She's really into being healthy. It's kind of annoying."

"What, did you want your dad marrying someone who's *un*healthy?" I say.

"No, it's just like she wants to rub it in my face that my mom had cancer. Like she's saying, 'I'll never have cancer because I'm the poster girl for health.'"

"I think you might be overthinking it," I offer.

"Or," Moe adds, "maybe your stepmom's trying to take care of herself so your dad won't lose another wife."

"She's twenty-nine," Elodie says. "It's not like she's going to suddenly die of leukemia."

"Just sayin'." Moe holds up a hand. "Cut the bitch a break."

Elodie rolls her eyes. "I just have no idea why my dad would go from her to *that*."

"Well, maybe he didn't want an exact replica," Moe says. "And that would be fucked up if he did, right?"

Elodie looks away, conceding.

"Besides," Moe adds, "you didn't want the guy to be alone forever, did you?"

I'm impressed at Moe's powers of intuition. I pick up

the photo to look at Moe's parents, and as I reach for it, Elodie points at my triceps.

"What happened to your arm?"

"Yikes. Nasty," Moe says.

They stare at the dark blue bruise. For a second I consider lying about it. Then I realize I'm enrolled in a rehab program where they claim that telling the truth supposedly helps you curb your bad habits.

"I got into a thing with Brady."

They stare at me for a minute before Elodie realizes. "He did that to you?"

"It was just a pinch."

"I knew that guy was a fucking dick," Moe says.

"How'd you know that?" I retort.

Moe looks away and shrugs. "I have an excellent dick detector."

"Has he done that before?" Elodie touches my arm. I don't want to answer her, but I remember at the Homecoming Dance in the fall, Brady got hammered and accused me of flirting with Greg Devorian. Greg was telling me about some rock-climbing trip in Wyoming he went on the year before. I'd been rock climbing once in Colorado with my family about six years ago, and it was one of the few times we'd all gotten along really well. My brother, Jake, would tell me ghost stories every night, and we'd do relay races on the hill outside our hotel. My mom and dad cuddled in the hotel room, and my dad taught Jake and me to fish. For once we were far away from everything, doing "family stuff," and it was nice.

When Brady came out of the bathroom, he saw me talking to Greg and he walked up and yanked me away. He'd been jealous of Greg ever since the guys on the lacrosse team started calling Greg "Horse" for reasons involving anatomical size and scope. Boys and their fragile, fragile egos. For a second, I'd had a naive hope that Horse might step forward to defend me or something, but he quickly backed away, disappearing into the crowd. That's when the toxic heft of my reputation became clear. I was Brady's girlfriend, and he could do whatever he wanted to me, even if it meant twisting my arm at a dance in front of half the school. Greg Devorian may have had a big dick, but at that moment his balls were nonexistent.

"That's, like, abuse," Elodie says softly after I tell them the story.

For once Moe is silent, appraising me with her brown eyes encased in black liquid eyeliner. She abruptly leans over to her desk and fidgets with her iPod.

"I know what's gonna cheer you up," she says. The sound of a Katy Perry song suddenly comes blasting out of the speakers on her desk.

"Are you serious?" Elodie laughs.

"Why, yes, I am," Moe says. She starts dancing in a hilariously rhythm-free manner, her cherry-red hair flying all over the place.

"Katy Perry sucks," I offer.

"I beg your pardon?" Moe speaks with mock offense as she bumps and grinds.

Elodie nods in agreement with me. "She's pretty bubblegum."

"What's wrong with bubblegum?" Moe asks.

"I thought your stoner goth friends listened to death punk or speed metal or whatever."

"Well, they do, but I love my pop music," Moe says. "Can you blame me when you hear this jam?" She does another little shimmy. "C'mon! Dance!"

I look at Elodie, who shrugs and stands up, giving Moe a hip bump. And suddenly Moe and Elodie and I are dancing to bubblegum as it blasts around us. And it's not so sucky after all.

Teenage Dream

Tabitha is cracking up
because Moe is doing the Jerk.
I break into the Dougie
and just then
a guy walks by the open door.
He is a few years older than us, maybe,
and he's tall and has floppy hair
and a Led Zeppelin T-shirt
and endless brown eyes
and he looks right at me
and Moe yells,
Get outta here!
And he looks at me
and says, *Nice Dougie,*
and walks off.

Who was that? Tabitha asks.
My brother, Moe says,
and they keep dancing.
I try to move,
but I am frozen in place
because other than Brady Finch,
I've never seen
a guy that handsome
in all my
teenage dreams.

TABITHA

JAMS

We bounce down the stairs, still singing that Katy Perry song. Without music to accompany her, Moe sounds like a dying goat, but she doesn't seem to care. It's kind of amazing how she's able to act like an idiot and be totally comfortable with it. I've been so caught up in needing my privacy I felt like I couldn't be myself. I had to be what everyone expected me to be. But here I can be whoever.

As I'm putting on my boots, Moe stops me.

"Wait. This is for you," Moe says, handing me a CD. "I burned it for you while we were listening to it. You need your own copy."

I look at the CD, which says BUBBLEGUM JAMS. It's the first time anyone's actually *made* me anything in a while. As a kid I had a rocking horse in my room that my dad built for me, but I always had a sneaking suspicion he bought it at a toy store. But I'm probably just paranoid.

"Thanks," I say.

"Don't let anyone hear you listening to it, because they might think you have no taste."

"Who cares?" I say. And it's the truth.

MOE'S PLAYLIST: BUBBLEGUM JAMS

"Greatest American Hero (Believe It or Not)"—*Joey Scarbury*

"Raise Your Glass"—*Pink*

"Born This Way"—*Lady Gaga*

"Crazy in Love"—*Beyoncé & Jay-Z*

"Crazy for You"—*Madonna*

"Girlfriend"—*Avril Lavigne*

"I Gotta Feeling"—*The Black Eyed Peas*

"Toxic"—*Britney Spears*

"Can't Get You Outta My Head"—*Kylie Minogue*

"Since U Been Gone"—*Kelly Clarkson*

"Teenage Dream"—*Katy Perry*

"Human Nature"—*Michael Jackson*

"When I Grow Up"—*The Pussycat Dolls*
"I Love Rock 'n' Roll"—*Joan Jett and the Blackhearts*
"Hollaback Girl"—*Gwen Stefani*
"Empire State of Mind"—*Jay-Z & Alicia Keys*
"Glory of Love"—*Peter Cetera*

Rhododendrons

As I walk down Moe's driveway
past the untended rhododendrons
and the geraniums that
look like they're on their last legs,
there's Moe's brother,
sitting on his bike
like he's waiting for something.
Hey, he says.
Oh, hey. I'm leaving, I offer lamely. *I'm late.*
For what? He smiles. *Got a hot date?*
I want to say something sassy,
but I know it will just come out dumb
so I say, *Maybe.*
I was right.
It did come out dumb.

*   *   *

Lucky guy, he says, which means he is definitely
  mocking me.
But then he looks right into my eye,
into my ocular nerve,
into the center of my cerebral cortex,
and I feel as dizzy as if I'd just pocketed a Hello Kitty
  alarm clock
or a clutch from Coach.

I panic. *Bye!*
I abruptly turn and walk away,
passing the rhododendrons
that now look like pink gemstones,
and the geraniums
that suddenly seem hopeful
and pearly and recently watered,
alive with grand ideas of things to come.

*MOE

APRIL 20

When I told Aunt B I had people over, she made a big show of saying how happy she was I had new friends. She looked at Marc and said, "What do you think? Did you get to meet them?" He didn't really respond and mumbled something, which is odd, since he usually has an opinion about everything. Usually a stupid opinion, but still an opinion. Then she asked me if I know Tabitha and Elodie from class and I said yeah and she asked which class and Marc looked curious too. I lied and said Social Studies because I couldn't tell them the real truth. They don't know about the shoplifting because when I got caught I told the security people at the store I was an orphan and they took pity on me. Even though it's true, I felt like a scumbag lying about that. But I knew Aunt B would worry. She and Marc already worry enough about me as it is. So the store agreed to sign me up for the class as my punishment, and if I went to all the classes, they wouldn't make the phone call.

Marc goes, "I thought you weren't taking Social Studies this semester," and I said, "Yes, I am," and he looked at me weird, but then Aunt B suggested we all go out to eat at Zeppo, which we haven't in weeks, so all's well that ends well, as Ms. Hoberman likes to say.

TABITHA

DOWN THE HALLWAY

As I leave Creative Writing, I fall in step with the mill of students drifting between classes, all chattering about the Spring Fling. Aptly so, because it feels like the perfect spring day, sunny and crisp. The Portland rains have made everything green, and the flowers by the gym are starting to pop open. It's one of those good high school moments, where everyone seems sort of in sync and for once, people aren't being annoying.

As I round the corner, I catch sight of a familiar cherry-red mop of hair, and eyes adorned with black eyeliner. She's walking in the opposite direction. We catch eyes, but the flow of traffic pushes us along, until Moe raises her hand. For a second I think she's going to wave at me, but instead she flips me the bird and keeps on going.

I can't help but laugh because I know she's joking, and

Sarah Crowder, an eager sophomore who's standing nearby getting a drink at the fountain, looks up happily, thinking I was laughing or smiling in her direction. I could correct her sorely mistaken assumption, but I just nod. Give the poor girl a thrill. Unfortunately, she takes it as an invitation to bound up to me.

"Hey, Tabitha! How's it going?" she chirps.

"Good. How are you?"

"I'm good." Then she adds, "I heard you and Brady broke up."

I look at her and almost want to tell her she's a dumb bitch and doesn't know jack shit about my life, because Brady and I haven't broken up, and who the hell told her that? I want to say this loudly and angrily, but then I remember what a perfect spring day it is and decide, *Why should I ruin that for someone else?*

"I haven't talked to him in a few days," I say, simply stating the truth. "Which is fine."

"Really?" she says, looking even more surprised than I feel. "What happened?"

"Oh, you know...it kind of fizzled out." I shrug, realizing that if everyone is gossiping about me, they might as well know the real story.

"Well," she says, "I don't know if it's okay to say this, but I think you can do better."

I think about it for a second, then say, "Thanks, Sarah. I appreciate that." Her friends are watching her, waiting to ask about every detail of our conversation. "See you around," I add, smiling at her and her friends as I pass, because there's nothing wrong with spreading a little joy now and then.

*MOE

APRIL 21

In European History today, Noah leaned over during Mr. Sussman's lecture about World War Whatever and asked me what I was doing later. I said, "It's anonymous," and turned back to Mr. Sussman as if learning about battles was the most important thing in my life. Noah doesn't have any friends in this class, so I guess he felt like it was okay to tap me on the shoulder and ask me that. There's something about his only wanting to talk to me when nobody else is around that's getting more and more irritating. Although it's probably not fair to be mad at him, because I'm not mad at Tabitha and Elodie for not broadcasting our friendship to everybody. But I don't make out with Tabitha or Elodie, so I guess that's the difference.

Photo Op

All you guys look great, Rachelle says
to the lacrosse team,
assembled for the yearbook photo.
Rachelle is "overseeing" the photo,
but really all she wants is face time with Dustin Diaz.
I fire off five quick shots, and the players scatter.
Did you get a good one? Rachelle says, and I nod.
She bolts over to Dustin like an attacker sprinting for the goal.
Hey, Brady Finch yells over to me.
He's got Jason Baines in a headlock.
Take a picture of me kicking Jason's ass.
Rachelle shoots me a look like *Great photo op!*
so I have no choice.
I put my eye to the lens,
but when the shutter snaps,

what I see isn't a perfect specimen of human anatomy;
it's merely the portrait of a douche bag.
So I turn and do something
I never thought I'd do.
I turn and walk away
from Brady Finch.

TABITHA

CAFETERIA

"These fish sticks are gross," Kayla says, frowning as she bites into one of them. We sit at our table with Samantha Bartle and a few of our other acquaintances.

"Then don't eat them," I say.

"I can't even tell what kind of fish this *is*." She pokes at it.

Just then, Taryn sits down and gives me a fake smile.

"Hey, T, whassup?" she coos.

If there is one question I truly hate, it's "What's up?" It's a total non-question. At least "How are you?" provides a topic to which you can easily offer an answer: "I'm fine," "I'm pissed off," "I'm great," "Not good," etc. "What's up?" requires people to rack their brains, trying to summon up a laundry list of all the things that might be "up." It's too much work for one lazy two-syllable question, and it pisses me off.

I choose to ignore the query altogether.

"Mackerel," I say to Kayla.

"What?"

"I bet it's mackerel in the fish sticks."

Kayla studies them, confused. "I don't even know what mackerel is."

"So, like I said, don't eat them."

Kayla sighs. "When is it going to be pizza day? They never have pizza anymore. Remember how Patrick was supposed to teach us to make pizza?"

At this moment, I see Brady walk into the cafeteria. He's heading this way, so I quickly stand up.

"Here," I say to Kayla. "Eat my hummus. It's made of garbanzo beans."

I quickly gather my tray and head out the back door, making what I hope is a dignified exit, but not really caring if it's all that dignified or not. The only thing I hear as I go is Kayla saying, "What the fuck is a garbanzo bean?"

TAUPE

"What do you think, the taupe or the salmon?" my mom asks me. She's sitting at the dining room table wearing a dress and heels and diamond hoop earrings. She flips through a catalog from Restoration Hardware as I pour myself a bowl of Special K for dinner.

"For what?" I ask.

"For the new blinds in the living room. It needs a spruce-up."

The front door opens and my dad enters, wearing a pin-striped suit and carrying his briefcase. He gives a tight smile when he sees us.

"What do you think, Jacob? Taupe or salmon?" But my dad's already past us and beelining for the sanctity of the bedroom.

"Honey?" my mom calls out. "Remember we have dinner with the Underwoods? They wanted to try that new Indian place downtown?"

"I have to go back to the office," my dad says. "I just came home to grab a change of clothes."

My mom nods and goes back to her catalog.

We sit in silence as he pads around upstairs, and then a few minutes later we hear him come downstairs, and then the front door closes with a gentle click.

I feel like there's nowhere I can be where there isn't a dickhead male polluting my airspace.

"I guess I can just have a bite here," my mom says. "I'll call Rachel to cancel. She'll understand."

I stare at her. Her once-beautiful face now has crow's-feet around her eyes and lines around her mouth. She's still pretty, and her blond hair looks sleek and perfect as always, but she's choking on the obvious.

"Seriously, Mom. Really?"

She looks up at me. "What?"

"Where is he even going?"

"He's going to work. Didn't you hear him say that?"

"It's seven thirty at night." I can't believe she's managed to live in such an utterly delusional state.

"I think the front room should be more muted," she says. "The salmon is tacky. I'm going with the taupe."

Good Eye

I pass my dad's office
on the way upstairs.
I poke my head in
and say, *Hey, how was your presentation?*
He looks surprised and says, *It was fine.*
Thank you for asking.
He's so formal
it's hard to tell what he's thinking
or if he's having fun talking or not,
but I guess he must be
because he asks how Yearbook is going
and I take out my camera and
show him a few photos.

*   *   *

You have a good eye, he says.
It's something my mom used to say.
She loved photography
as much as she loved movies
and, I guess, as much as she loved me
or as much as she loved him.
We catch each other's gaze for a second
and he says, *You must miss her a lot.*
I don't want to talk about it
so I bolt out, saying, *I'd better get back to my homework.*
He says, *I'll see you downstairs,*
and we part ways
as friends,
or whatever it is
you want to call it.

APRIL 22

Today after Shoplifters Anonymous we took the bus to Multnomah Village to the Vinyl Monkey. It just opened next to Switch Shoes on Capitol Highway, and it's a good spot to hang out, since no one cares about records anymore and the people who go there are older and cool. It would be a great place to steal from too, except it's not exactly easy to fit an LP under your shirt and go unnoticed. Flat, square boobs would be pretty obvious. Plus, the lady who owns it is really nice. She's in her fifties and skinny and she wears colorful muumuus and somehow makes them seem stylish. In addition to the orange clogs she sports, her best quality is she has a genuine love of pop songs. To Alex and Janet, any pop song or body movement beyond a head nod that a song might inspire is considered a colossal social foul. I don't know why they are so anti-dancing, but it sucks.

Today Lady turned up the music really loud and we shimmied around the store. I greatly enjoyed doing the Sprinkler, and Elodie and Tabitha showed real promise Washing the Car.

On the walk back to Nob Hill afterward, Marc's name came up and Elodie got all blushy. She obviously has a crush on him. I've only known two girls he's dated, but he broke up with them because he said he wanted a girl with a good heart. Even though I don't know Elodie all that well, I'd say that if anyone fits the "good heart" bill, it's probably her.

Everybody Else

After the record store
we go to the MAC store in Nob Hill
and Tabitha says, *Let's get some fake eyelashes.*
Why would we want those? Moe asks.
Because, Tabitha explains,
you ask them to put the lashes on for you
and then you ask for a little bit of concealer
and a little bit of eyeliner
and then bam,
you've gotten a free makeover.

As the guy does my lashes, I can't help but wonder
if Marc will think I look good.
Tabitha leaves us there and after a while
comes back with a pair of earrings.

One is a star and the other is a moon.
She hands them to Moe.
That's a thank-you for the mix CD, Tabitha says.
Moe grins as she puts them in her ears.
Did you steal these?
Tabitha tells her, *Of course.*
She knows stolen gifts mean way more
than ones that are bought,
because of what you have to go through
to get them.
We only have three meetings left, she says,
so we'd better work our magic while we still can.
I guess that was her way
of saying that once this is over,
it's over.

Speaking in Code

You look nice,
Jenna says to me when I come home,
and I say, *Thanks*, but what I really want to ask is:
"Is that code for 'You normally look ugly'?"
But I don't.
What's the occasion? she asks.
(Code for: "Do you actually have a life?")
I tell her, *No occasion. I was out with some friends.*
(Code for: "Fuck you very much.")
Girlfriends or guy-friends? ("I love being nosy.")
Girls, I say. ("Must we continue this conversation?")
Oh, that's nice, she says. ("You're a loser.")
I know them from Shoplifters Anonymous, I add.
("I'm a dangerous criminal, so don't mess with me.")
How's Rachelle? she asks. ("I thought you only had one
    friend.")
I shrug and say, *Fine*. ("Can we stop talking now?")
So are there any guys at school you like? she asks.
("Is there a remote possibility you'll ever have a
    boyfriend?")
Not really. ("Would I tell you if I did?")
I'll call you when dinner's ready, she offers. ("I give up.")
Sounds good, I say. ("We will never, ever be friends, so
    please stop trying.")

*MOE

APRIL 24

Today in the parking lot I saw Noah getting into his car so I decided SCREW IT and I walked up to him. I was about to say hi when he goes, "Are you confusing me with someone else?" And then I saw that Kayla Lee and another girl were already sitting in the backseat, staring out at me.

I was so pissed. When I came home, the parrot kept squawking like he felt my pain. Then about a half hour later the doorbell rang and it was Noah. I tried to shut the door in his face, but he stopped me and said, "Here," and went to hand me a Kit Kat bar. A fucking Kit Kat?! He started to say something, but I slammed the door in his face. Afterward I just stood there with my heart beating really fast. I waited for a few minutes, then opened the front door. He was gone, but he'd left the Kit Kat bar on the front mat. We have this really stupid mat that says "HOWDY, STRANGER!" with a squirrel in a cowboy hat on it, and it was sitting in the middle of that.

I realized that this was the first time he had ever come to the front door of my house. And I was about to throw the Kit Kat into the front yard when I remembered the very first time we ever talked, way back when I moved here, when I was in fourth grade. I was outside sitting on the curb, taking a break from lugging all my shit inside, and I was eating a Kit Kat. He rode by on his bike and stopped and asked me if I was moving in. And I said, "Duh." But he looked so sad that I felt guilty and offered him some of my Kit Kat. He ate it with a huge smile and that was the beginning of the end for me and Noah Simos.

SIZE:

PART FIVE

5824583647 38824039

"*Why does every encounter with the one person I want to impress seem to involve humiliation?*"

Live Forever

I go grocery shopping with Jenna at New Seasons
for coconut water and brown rice,
gluten-free this and paraben-free that,
and oodles and oodles of kale.
Jenna's ten years younger than my dad
so she's always buying food
that will make him "live forever."
I think she considers a trip to New Seasons
to be one of our many attempts at bonding—
every single one of which has fallen flat.

When we go outside
some BMX guys are in the parking lot
in front of Great Clips.

One of them is doing some kind of wheelie
and another guy's riding faster than most cars go,
and as he speeds by,
I see it's Moe's brother, Marc.
Do those guys go to your school? Jenna asks.
I say yes and she says, *They seem like bad news.*
The psychologist I went to when my mom died
would call that a "projection":
when you say someone is "bad news"
because you actually believe it about yourself.

All I know is that Marc is doing some kind of trick
where he rides up on one of those cement parking space
    thingies
and flies up into the air
and as he does, I pull out my camera and snap
    a photo.
Jenna doesn't notice, so I pocket my Canon
and glance back over at him
and that's when I walk into the cart,
which smacks into another cart,
which hits another cart,
and then they all start rolling down the little hill
and the bikers have to pedal out of the way.
Marc spots me standing there,
so I give Lame Wave #2
and pray that aliens will immediately invade
    Earth

and export me elsewhere
so I don't have to endure the humiliation
of my stepmother watching me
being watched by a boy
I am pretending not to see.

TABITHA

REDECORATION

At my mom's insistence, we've been shopping all Saturday for a new rug for the living room. She has moved off salmon and taupe and is now gravitating toward teal and gold.

"I don't know why you're so obsessed with redecorating," I say. "Didn't you just redo it a year ago?"

"It makes me happy," she says, slapping down her AmEx for a $9,300 Persian that complements her new color scheme.

It may make her happy, but it makes me kind of sick. Although who am I to talk? My shoplifting probably makes her just as ill.

Afterward my mom has an appetite. We go to Fratelli in the Pearl for lunch, and she orders the market fish and a vodka tonic. As the waiter is delivering our drinks, I see Kayla and Taryn heading toward us, loaded down with shopping bags. Fuck.

"Tabs? How are you?" Taryn says.

"Where have you been?" Kayla asks, hugging me hello.

"Just busy with homework," I say. I haven't spoken to them in three days. Ever since I confirmed to Sarah Crowder that Brady and I had "fizzled out." Word was out. I had been avoiding their fervent texts and dodging them at the lockers.

"We saw you yesterday at MAC," Taryn says, glancing at me sideways. "Who were those girls you were with?"

"Wasn't she with you guys?" my mom asks, taking a sip of her drink. Balls. That's what I'd told her.

"No, she was with, like"—Taryn pauses—"people we don't know."

"New friends!" My mom claps, excited.

Kayla looks at me. "I think I've seen the one with the red hair around?"

This is a nightmare.

"No idea. We met at SAT class." I shrug, trying to play it cool.

"You won't call us back, so we went dress shopping without you." Taryn glares at me.

"She got a black Miu Miu," adds Kayla. "Mine's a white Max Mara with a yellow sash. So seasonal, right?"

"Are you girls coming over to get ready?" my mom asks. "We had so much fun last year."

"It would have been more fun if I hadn't gotten my period that night. I totally soaked through my panties, remember?" Kayla says to me, cringing.

"Yeah, that was not good," I agree.

"I don't know why you would get white again." Taryn shoots an eye-roll at Kayla.

"Ooh! We could rent a limo for you guys!" my mom enthuses.

"Can we talk about this later?" I say to her.

Taryn stares info-gathering lasers into my face. "Are you going with Brady?"

I don't have an answer, so I just shrug. "I have no idea."

"I'll take another one of these," my mom says, holding up her empty glass to the passing waiter.

"A limo sounds fun," Kayla says.

Taryn looks less certain, so she changes the subject. "We gotta roll. We're meeting my mom and dad at valet. Call me," she says, pulling Kayla away as she waves good-bye.

After they leave, my mom looks at me. "Who are the new friends they were talking about?"

I take a deep breath. "From that shoplifting program."

"Oh." She raises an eyebrow, surprised. "So you lied."

"It's less hassle that way."

"So if we did the limo, you wouldn't want them to come too?"

"They're not really the limo types."

She nods. Then says, "Well, never mind. Your father thinks limos are ostentatious anyway. He'd hate me spending money on something like that."

"What about a Persian rug?"

"That's different," she says, smoothing her hair. "It's an investment. A limo is a frivolity."

"Why are you so worried about pissing him off? Who cares?" I retort.

My mom avoids the question. The waiter arrives and sets down her fresh cocktail.

"Aren't you upset he's cheating on you?" I press. I can't help it. It just comes out.

She gives me a sharp stare. "That isn't really your business, Tabitha."

"Well, he's my dad," I say loudly. "I live there too."

"Shh!" my mom whispers. But I don't care if anyone hears—the waiter, or the old couple next to us, or even the slender redhead two tables over. I noticed her right when we walked in. And it wasn't the first time I'd seen her. I saw her a year ago at a club called Aura, on Burnside. I snuck in with Brady and some of his friends. Brady had gotten me the worst fake ID in the world, and it was a miracle we didn't get thrown out. Brady wanted to go crash the VIP section, so we did, and that's when I saw the redhead, sitting there with my dad. She had to be twenty-two, at the oldest. I was tipsy on Jaeger shots we'd done earlier in the park, so I pulled a waitress aside and asked her to send my dad a drink. I watched as the waitress took the drink over to his table. She set it down, I saw his expression, and as the waitress turned around to point me out, I lost my nerve and ran—leaving to my imagination the look on my father's face as he stared at a Shirley Temple in total confusion.

*MOE

APRIL 26

Last night Alex and Janet came to pick me up. My aunt was working the night shift, so she couldn't bitch about me going out with inappropriate friends. Noah was in front of his house. He saw me climbing into Alex's beat-up Chevy all dressed up, rocking fishnet stockings. I glared at him and he stared back, looking kind of bummed. When I shut the door, Alex goes, "Nice fishnets. I didn't know you were into the tranny whore look." I laughed it off, but it kind of hurt my feelings. I'm normally the one who makes fun of people, and I have to say I don't like it when the tables are turned. Then she asked me who the lax bro across the street was, and I said I didn't know. And she said lax bros are tools. I didn't want to ruin the night so I just let her and Janet talk crap about "assholes like that." I kept telling myself to keep calm and stay quiet, because Noah is none of their business.

*   *   *

The party was for some older guys Janet knew who gradu-
ated a few years ago and now basically just deal drugs.
Alex has a crush on one of the guys, Gabe, and when we
were standing out by the bonfire doing whiskey shots,
Gabe's friend said I was hot. I turned to Alex and was like,
"Good news, apparently the tranny whore look is in. Maybe
you should rethink your homeless lesbian wardrobe." I
have a feeling that was the liquid courage talking, so I kept
drinking and before I knew it, I couldn't find her anymore,
which meant she either left without me or went upstairs to
have sex with Gabe. Neither of which were options I cared
to think about too much.

Some guy who seemed all amped up on happy pills offered
to give me a ride home, but I try to avoid one-on-one time
with future date rapists. I couldn't call Marc. He'd freak
out. So that left only one person nice enough and sober
enough for me to drunk dial in the middle of the night.

Elodie

SOS

HELP! COME GET ME!!!!
Nobody's ever texted me at 3:00 AM before.
I stare at my phone,
all bleary, before seeing it's Moe.
WHERE R U? I write.
She writes back: FELONY FLATS.
I lie there, pondering my escape,
then finally get up, slide on my slippers,
and sneak out of my room
using the light from my phone
as my own little lightsaber.
I slip down the hallway
and thank God I've got skills as a thief.
I crawl into the master bedroom
at the opposite end of the hall

and ever so quietly
grab my dad's keys off the dresser
and in slow motion
I crawl out,
freezing on my knees when I hear him roll over,
but fortunately he keeps sleeping
so I tiptoe downstairs,
out the front door,
down the driveway,
and get in the car
and go.

Drive

I feel like an action-hero car thief,
like I am Ryan Gosling in *Drive*
about to speed his way out of trouble.
I don't have a driver's license yet,
but my dad gave me driving lessons a few months ago,
before he knew I was a delinquent.
I start the car and switch it into gear
and make it down the driveway in reverse.
I've never driven at night, let alone illegally.
If I'm caught now,
the cops will probably send me to jail
or my parents will make go to military school.
I could go to prison.
Those thoughts alone
should stop me from doing it,
but somehow danger
is an excellent motivator.
Shawn never talks about it in class,
but the truth is, being scared makes you feel more alive
than regular living.
You can feel your lungs expanding and your heart
    pumping
and your corpuscles contracting.
I read in a magazine that sex makes you feel alive too,
but since I've never had it,
this is as good as it gets.

Ember

When I get to Felony Flats,
I see Moe sitting on the curb
in front of a run-down house
with a bunch of old furniture on the lawn
and heavy metal blasting.
The only thing visible is the small flame of her cigarette.
She is an ember burning in the dark
in fishnets.
When I get closer, I see a hole in the netting.
She crawls into the car.
You're here, she says with a sigh,
and falls into my shoulder.
Thanks, El.
She has that boozy smell, the one my dad had for days
after my mom's funeral,
before he woke up one day
and went back to work,
met a secretary in the PR department,
married her,
and never looked back.

Moe puts her feet up on the dash.
What happened to you? I ask
She just shrugs
and I take the cigarette out of her hand
before it burns the seat.

I could chuck it,
but instead I take a puff and
hold it in a second before I realize
I have no idea what I'm doing.
I cough and cough and
Moe starts laughing.
What?! I say. *I've never smoked before!*
Keep it that way, she says,
and grabs it out of my hand, throws it out the window,
and we drive on,
leaving it there to burn.

Lack of Personal Grooming

When we get to Moe's,
Marc is waiting out front
and he's pissed.
What the fuck, Moe?
You just swore, Moe giggles.
Sorry about this, I say to him,
nervously tucking my hair behind an ear.
Why don't I have any lip gloss on?
Or mascara?
Why am I wearing pajamas with cartoon drawings
of pieces of cherry pie on them?
Why am I not wearing a bra,
but I am wearing a blob of Proactiv
on the zit on my forehead?
I furiously try to rub it off,
realizing I have absolutely no idea
what my breath smells like and
he looks at me and smiles.
Thanks for picking her up.
I smile back, as does my pimple,
which is so big it probably has a mouth of its own.
You two are precious, Moe slurs as she climbs out of
    the car.
I follow after her with one of her boots,
wishing I could bonk her over the head with it.

A Gentleman and a Lady

I love you, Elodie, Moe says
as Marc and I tuck her into bed.
It makes me want to hit her a little less hard.
We tiptoe down the hall, trying to be extra quiet
so her aunt and the parrot won't wake up.
Marc walks me out to the car and says, *Nice pj's.*
I look down and see a huge spaghetti sauce stain
on one of my pieces of cherry pie.
Why does every encounter
with the one person I want to impress
seem to involve humiliation?

But then he leans forward to open the door
and puts me inside like I am precious cargo.
You're cute at four in the morning, he says,
and I have no idea what to say back
other than *You too*
and I start to buckle my seat belt,
but he grabs my hand and holds it for a second
and I look up into his endless brown eyes
and then he steps back, letting me go.

I back out of the driveway,
my pimple and I only hitting one pothole as we go.
He's still watching so I give an idiotic little salute
and keep driving
in my cherry-pie pajamas

with a stupid smile on my face
still feeling his hand in my hand
all the way home
and into my driveway
and into the house
and down the hall
and into bed
where I lie
until the sun comes up
and the alarm goes off
and I'm still thinking
about the night before.

*MOE

APRIL 28

I brought Elodie a bunch of chocolate to SA as a thank-you for saving my life. When Shawn asked what it was for, we said we were doing an Identification Exercise, which made her practically pee with excitement.

After class we went to Tabitha's house, which was HUGE and glass, with views of the valley. There was no one home. It was kind of like a museum where you thought a security guard might rush over and grab you if you touched anything. Tabitha showed us a bunch of blogs. Some were just people's thoughts about music or movies they like or their Tumblrs and she showed us the one made by the girl our age who's all into finding cool old stuff in your mom's closet that could be used for new fashion looks and whatnot.

As we were leaving, Elodie told us it was her birthday tomorrow, which is so weird because everyone loves to brag about their birthday, but leave it to Elodie to wait and say something when it's too late to do anything about it. Her dad got her a big gift certificate to Nordstrom and she said she wants to take us "shopping." We all had a good laugh over it. I have an idea of the perfect thing to get her, but for now, Tabitha and I did a funny pre-birthday dance set to the tune of Willow Smith's "Whip My Hair." Elodie was lying on the floor laughing so hard she farted, so I think it was a successful present.

When I got home I asked Aunt B if I could borrow some cool old clothes from her closet, and she called me a "smart-ass." I tried to explain to her I wasn't joking, I was trying to become more fashionable, but she didn't believe me. Proving once again that my reputation leaves something to be desired.

TABITHA

PIZZA DAY

Patrick Cushman looks kind of surprised when I sit down next to him at his lunch table. He's sitting there eating a sandwich with a group of band kids.

"Happy pizza day," I say.

A guy stops polishing his oboe. They all stare at me in surprise.

"You're kind of hard to find," I say to Patrick, pressing a napkin on the molten piece of greasy cheese pizza. I'm trying to absorb whatever liquid is sitting on top.

"How's that?" he asks, watching me with amusement.

"You never sit at the same table."

"I like to mix it up," he says, nonchalant.

"Smart move," I say. A freckly girl from my gym class nods at me. "Hey, Laura," I volunteer as I wad up the greasy napkin and put it in the corner of my tray.

Then I turn back to Patrick. "So, do you really make this pizza at home?" I cut a tiny piece off with my knife and put it in my mouth. It's like somewhat digestible wet rubber mixed with somewhat digestible dry rubber. I manage to chew. Barely.

"He watches me swallow. "I can't believe you just allowed that to enter your body."

I immediately regret consuming it. "It's probably going to live in my intestines for twenty years, isn't it?"

"Fifty," he says. "Here. Try this. It's much better. I don't actually make pizza, but I do make a mean sandwich." He hands me half of a turkey on whole wheat. It's got some sort of sprouts and tomato on it.

"I thought you were into pizza."

"I told you—I like to mix it up."

I appraise the turkey sandwich. "This better be good."

"Just trust me," he says, and smiles at me. I bite into it and chew. It's delicious.

Birthday Present

I'm up in my room
hating trigonometry more than life itself
when Jenna knocks on my door.
Someone's here to see you.
I go downstairs
and standing there on my front porch
is Marc Truax.
He's wearing a black Nirvana T-shirt
and scuffed Vans
and I am literally speechless.
It's a good thing he is able to speak.
Happy birthday, he says,
followed by,

Do you want to go for a walk?
And I nod yes
and Jenna tries to act like
she's not full-on eavesdropping,
but I'm so happy I don't even care.

Turning Sixteen

Marc says there's a rad doughnut place
that we could go to.
I'm not really sure what the big deal about doughnuts is,
but it doesn't matter
because before I know it,
we're walking
near the Burnside Bridge
and talking
and I'm nervous being around him
but only for about five minutes
and pretty soon
we're talking about everything;
I tell him about my old school
and my mom
and he talks about motorcycles from the seventies,
which of course I know nothing about,
and finally we get to this really awesome bakery
called Voodoo
and they're playing cool music
and the girl behind the counter
is all pierced and friendly
and Marc asks for one doughnut dusted with Tang
and another one topped with Cap'n Crunch
and I get chocolate on chocolate,
but before we eat them,
he says, *Hang on,*
and buys me a pair of underwear

with the Voodoo logo and a slogan
that says THE MAGIC IS IN THE HOLE.
I blush, since no guy has ever bought me doughnuts, let
    alone underwear.
Then he pulls a candle out of his pocket
that looks kind of used
and he goes, *Sorry, it was the only one I could find.*
I had to mug somebody for it.
He grins and lights it
and he and the girl behind the counter
sing "Happy Birthday" really loud.
I make my wish,
which is you-know-what,
and we sit there devouring doughnuts
and when we're done
he buys me a bunch more to take home.
He says if I'm celebrating my birthday properly,
I need to have enough to last a whole week,
because you can't just turn sixteen once
and call it a day.

Doughnuts

What's this?
my dad asks when he sees the pink box on the counter
that says GOOD THINGS COME IN PINK BOXES.
Jenna says, *Doughnuts from Elodie's friend.*
Oh, he says.
A guy friend, she adds.
Oh, he says again.
He is clueless,
which is good
because if she blabs any more
I might start to get annoyed.

But when my dad gets up to go to his office,
she leans over and whispers,
I always liked bad boys too,
and I say, *He's not actually bad.*
And she says, *That's even better.*
It's weird: I never pictured Jenna at my age,
but obviously she once was,
before she grew up
and found a nice widower to marry
who happened to have a daughter
with whom she had nothing in common
until now.

*MOE

APRIL 29

After school Marc and I played Rage and when I teased him about Elodie, he made a point to slaughter five Gingers really fast right in a row, so I laid off. Then he asked me what Elodie was like. I said she was really sweet and a little shy but a good friend. I left out the part about how we met.

We went back to playing for a few minutes and then I asked him, "So are you into her or what?" and he said, "I'm just glad she's nice to my little sister," and went up to his room. For a second it was weird to think my brother and my friend might be dating, but then I realized what an adorable couple they'd make.

Speaking of (NOT) COUPLES, I haven't seen Noah since the night of Gabe's party. I want to run across the street and bang on Noah's windows, but it's not really my style, so I'll just sit here and think about how much it sucks we can't hang out and how much I hate him even though I don't.

TABITHA

MEMOIRS

"You guys did a great job on your memoirs," says Ms. Hoberman as she starts passing back our papers. I'm a little nervous because I wasn't going to write one, but after I talked to Elodie and Moe, it seemed a little less daunting—everybody's parents are crazy, so what's the big deal? Plus, once I started, I unleashed the beast and vented about my dad and all his bullshit, not to mention my mom refusing to stand up to him. Then I retyped it and added in a part about how my mom keeps redecorating our house ever since my brother went off to college. I wrote about how she thinks if she keeps buying new stuff, it will fix everything in our lives. I don't know if it made any sense, but at least it was the truth.

When Ms. H drops my paper on my desk, I see the A+

right at the top. I can't help but feel a little proud, especially when she says, "You did a lovely job, Tabitha." It seems like she wants to say more. Or maybe she wants to tell me that even though I'm talented, I may need therapy.

She gives back Patrick Cushman's paper and says, "Very nice writing, Patrick." I see the A on his, and he looks over at me and says, "I guess we're awesome, huh?"

I smile a little.

"So...what do you think about going to the Spring Fling thingamajig with me?" He says "Spring Fling thingamajig" in a self-effacing way, like he's trying to mock it, but obviously he's serious. It shocks the shit out of me. I mean, he's cute and nice, but Spring Fling? I think about how every relationship I've ever had seems to suck. Patrick Cushman deserves better than that. He deserves to have a great time at the Spring Fling with someone who is easy and simple and not complicated.

"I wish I could," I say. "But it's probably too messy of a situation."

His smile disappears. "What do you mean?" I want to say, *Even though you're not technically my type and you're the last person I'm supposed to go to the Fling with, I think you're kind of awesome*. But I don't. Instead, I shrug and say, "With Brady and everything." He looks hurt, and I feel like a dick. It used to be a feeling I was semi-comfortable with. But now it makes me as itchy as that sweater I used to love all through middle school, which, for some reason, suddenly started giving me hives until finally I had to throw it away.

DRESSES

I flip through the rainbow of dresses at Betsey Johnson. I don't know why I'm here, because I'm not going to the Fling with anyone, so I don't even need a dress. All I know is I'm on a weird kind of autopilot. I may look like any other customer on the outside, but inside I'm dangerous. Okay, maybe not dangerous like Moe or her friends are, but I'm definitely not happy.

I take an armful of clothes into the dressing room, carefully hiding two of them; when the salesgirl checks to see how many items I have, she gives me a tag that says "4" instead of "6." Inside, I try on a gauzy orange-and-yellow V-neck. Maybe Brady's right. Maybe I am a few pounds overweight.

In the hall today before sixth period I saw Zoe Amato and Keith Savage. She was gazing up at him as he pulled her in for a kiss. I look in the mirror and wonder if I'll ever find a guy who'll love me in the orange-and-yellow top the way Keith Savage loves Zoe Amato with her split ends and her flared jeans and her crooked bottom teeth.

"Everything okay in there?" the salesgirl calls.

"Yeah. Thanks," I say.

"Well, let me know if you need any other sizes."

"Okay."

I pull off the top and appraise the red dress. It's kind of like the one I stole months ago when Moe and Elodie and I first started stealing together, back when we first met. I carefully remove the sensor with nail clippers. If you clip it at just the right spot at the base, it won't burst open and spill its blue ink everywhere. It takes practice, that's all. I make sure not to snag the fabric before folding it and placing it inside my bag.

As I walk out, I leave a top on the floor and I hand the number "4" tag and the four items back to the salesgirl. Like I said, dangerous. Not to anybody else, just to myself.

Pipe Dream

I'm supposed to meet Moe and Tabitha in fifteen minutes
at the Car Wash fountain.
They're expecting me to bring something good
because Tabitha is stealing a halter top and jeans
and Moe is stealing an iPod
from some store on SW Fifth.
All I have so far is a photo book
about seventies motorcycle gear.
Okay, fine. It's for Marc.
I know I should be stealing what I told them I was going
   to steal
and not a book from River Books & Gifts
for a guy who's not even close to being my boyfriend.
Normally, we hate stealing from mom-and-pop shops,
but in this case the owners are assholes—

their anti-gay-marriage signs posted in the front window
    prove it—
so they deserve to get lifted.
I walk out, the book tucked under a copy of *The Merc*,
and I scoot down the sidewalk,
passing the new Apple Store.
I stop when I see
Moe through the window.
And she's not shoplifting at all:
She's standing at the front,
swiping her card into the iPad at the counter,
paying for stuff
she was supposed to be stealing.

Fake Like You

What's wrong? Tabitha asks when I get to the fountain.
I just saw Moe in the new Apple Store, I say.
She stole from Apple*?!* Tabitha freaks out.
She'll totally get caught!
No, I say, correcting her.
She wasn't stealing—she was buying.
Tabitha looks confused.
*Wasn't she supposed to take an iPod from that place on
    Fifth?*
I nod, trying to process the Why
and the What Next.

Hey, dudes, Moe says, walking up.
She pulls the iPod out of her bag.
Mission accomplished.
Tabitha glances at me.
Where'd you get this? she asks Moe.
That anti-gay place, Moe says, smug.
You stole it? I ask.
Moe rolls her eyes. *Of course I did.*
Tabitha and I look at each other.
Can we go? Moe says.
I don't want to hang around here waiting to get caught.

TABITHA

UNTIED

"Moe, wait. She just saw you buy it," I say.

Moe stops walking.

For the first time since I've known her, she looks uncertain. She bends down and reties the lace of her boot, even though it isn't untied.

I glare at her. "Why were you in Shoplifters Anonymous if you don't steal?"

"I steal," she says, defensive.

"But why were you buying something you said you were going to shoplift?" Elodie asks.

"Can't a person change her mind?" Moe backpedals.

"Wait a minute." I realize something. "All those other times—were you actually stealing, or were you just *saying* you were stealing?"

Elodie whips around to glare at me. "She wouldn't do that."

"Oh, come on," I retort. "You probably would have done it too. You were so desperate to be friends with me, you would have done anything."

"What?!" Elodie looks stung.

"Oh my God, you're pathetic," Moe snarls at me.

"I may have wanted to be your friend," Elodie says. "But (a) that's not a crime, and (b) I wouldn't have lied like Moe did in order to do it."

"Oh, wow. Low blow." Moe glares at Elodie.

"Well, whatever," I say, looking at both of them. "I wasn't *masquerading* as a shoplifter."

Moe snorts. "Masquerading is better than being a complete bitch."

This from a total phony who hangs out with grindcore vandals but loves covertly listening to Katy Perry.

"I agree," Elodie says.

"At least I'm not a loser like the two of you are," I say.

After I say it, I wish I could take it back. But it's too late. Elodie turns and marches off across SW Fifth and past the City Grill.

"Nice," Moe says, glaring at me before turning and walking in the opposite direction toward the 76 station, leaving me standing there alone, with nowhere to go but home.

SIZE:
PART SIX

5824583647 38824039

"People disappear, but objects stay."

*MOE

APRIL 30

I don't know if it was worth it to go and get friends I actually care about. But I guess if they were real friends, they wouldn't care if I stole an iPod or bought it. I should be able to tell them the sky is magenta or whatever, and they should believe me.

When I got home Marc asked me again about Elodie. I wanted to say she fooled me. I wanted to say that the reason I never let myself have real friends is because eventually they always let you down.

So I told him Elodie's a wimp who doesn't stand up for people. And she's a shoplifter. I probably should have also added that I lied to her and she called me on it, but instead I just pushed him out of my room and shut the door before he could see me cry.

TABITHA

THE HANDSOME STRANGER

I always wake up early; I can't help it. Maybe it's a trait I inherited from my dad. But today I'm not getting up early, because I didn't really sleep last night. All I did was lie there with a sick, anxious feeling.

I drag myself out of bed and pull on my jogging clothes and put my hair in a ponytail. The sun streams into my room, and I look around at the collection of snow globes, all the earrings and clothes. Almost every bit of it was procured with a five-finger discount. But even if it was achieved illegally, at least I have a bunch of trinkets to comfort me. People disappear, but objects stay.

"Hi, honey."

I turn around to see my dad standing in the doorway. It's been so many days since I've seen him, it's like he's a handsome stranger.

"Hey."

"How's school?" he asks, giving me an encouraging smile.

"Decent."

"And Brady?"

"Over." I shrug.

He nods without comment and picks up one of the snow globes from my bureau. Inside it is a little gingerbread house with a tiny oak tree in its yard. It was one of the first things I ever stole, three years ago from a stationery store in Beaverton. I remember how I plotted its theft, how clever I felt as my mom cluelessly drove us away from the scene of the crime.

"Sorry I've been working so late. I've been wanting to talk to you," he says, juggling the globe a little, creating a mini snowstorm.

"You do?" I can't help but feel a pang of excitement. Maybe this is the moment he comes clean about what he really does late at night. Maybe this is the moment the family bullshit can finally stop.

"I wanted to remind you to get your car serviced," he says.

I stare at him. That's what he has to talk to me about? A week ago I would have wanted to scream and shout and punch him for disappointing me. But now I realize it's better to take a deep breath and not say anything. The best thing I can do is stop expecting anything from him.

So I just say, "Okay, I'll do it this weekend."

He nods and backs out of the doorway.

I stand there for a second, stomach churning, watching the snow in the globe fall on the tiny cottage and the miniature tree as they sit in their bubble of glass, trapped in winter forever.

Natural Disaster

In Rachelle's world, closing the yearbook issue
is like running a tsunami crisis center.
She fancies herself at the center of everything,
staving back the rising water.
She's so stressed
not even Dustin Diaz has the power to save her from peril.
I try to stay out of the way
as she yells, *Where the hell is the French Club photo?!*
I want to tell her I gave it to her a week ago,
but that would only cause more destruction.
There is only one source of salvation
and he's walking past the window right now.
Hang on a second, I say, and dash out the door,
not caring that there's a gale force of Rachelle at my back
screaming my name.

Cold

Marc!
He stops when he sees me
and I'm suddenly horrified
because I've just chased a senior onto
   the sidewalk
in front of an entire room of Yearbook
   nerds.
I want to throw up
but instead I wait for our eyes to meet.
When they finally do
it's not a brown brown warmth
but a steely, dark cloud.
Have you talked to my sister? he asks.
I can feel Rachelle watching through the
   window,
wondering what the hell we're talking about
and if she should be recording it for local
   broadcast.
We got into a fight, I say.
Why? he asks.
Then he adds,
So you're a shoplifter, huh?
I stand there trying to muster a response
when he suddenly says, *I gotta go,*
and walks off, taking his brown brown
   eyes with him,

the frayed edge of his jeans,
the hole in his T-shirt
and the peek of his cocoa-y skin underneath,
as everything warm
grows cold.

*MOE

MAY 1

Today Alex, Janet, Roy, and I ditched school. We went to Roy's house and got high with his Sid Vicious bong and sat on his orange shag carpet and listened to the Circle Jerks. I don't know why I got so baked. I don't usually like pot, but sometimes drugs can be an acquired taste. This wasn't one of them. It didn't work for oysters either. No matter how many times I choke down those slimy things, I still want to hurl. As for the pot, all I felt was paranoid and like I had to pee every five minutes. Then Roy and Janet wanted to go outside and skateboard in the driveway, which just made me think about how if I hadn't whined about wanting a skateboard for my birthday, maybe my parents would never have gone to Big 5 that day and gotten into a car crash. If I'd been hanging out with Elodie and Tabitha, I'd have told them about all the thoughts that were flying around in my head; instead, I just sat there hoping I wasn't saying them out loud.

So, yeah. I don't really love getting high and listening to thrash punk. Maybe if they listened to something to dance to, I'd have stayed, but when Janet said it would be rad to watch *Pootie Tang* for the twentieth time, it gave me a good excuse to go home.

TABITHA

EVIL

Ms. Hoberman is losing it. Her signed and laminated *Romeo and Juliet* program is missing. It disappeared this morning from its place of honor above her desk.

"Maybe I should be happy that someone valued their field-trip experience so much they needed a permanent keepsake," Ms. Hoberman says. "But I'm not."

Yikes. Ms. Hoberman doesn't usually get so testy.

"I'm hoping whoever took it will return it immediately so I won't have to feel angry anymore."

I feel bad for Ms. Hoberman. She always goes out of her way to be nice to everybody, even the dickheads and the miscreants, so I'm not really sure why anyone would want to screw with her.

* * *

After class I head for my locker to pick up a Social Studies book, but when I see Brady and the gang hanging out there, I take shelter behind the snack machine and slip out the other way. Luckily, I make it the rest of the day without seeing them, until my mom comes to pick me up from school. I find her idling in the parking lot in her beige Lexus. She came to get me because my car's in the shop.

"You're on time," I say.

"Of course," she says. She seems sober, which is a relief. We don't need another arrest in the family.

As I climb inside and pull the door shut behind me, she says, "I saw Brady. Are you not together anymore?"

"Why do you ask?" I look away.

"He seemed cozy with your friend Taryn." That's news to me, but I certainly don't want to deal with it here and now.

"So what? Dad gets cozy with other women, right? No biggie."

Her face falls, and I immediately feel like an asshole.

"Sorry," I say. "That was evil."

She straightens up and says, "I chose a credenza for the living room. It's a lovely blond wood that will go really well with the new rug."

She puts the Lexus in gear, turns to me, and adds, "You know what? That *was* evil." And, without further ado, she drives us away.

MAY 2

It's raining again and cold and Aunt B yelled at me for not taking out the trash and Marc is grumpy. So basically everything is shitty. But I'm secretly trying to make it right. I hope it works.

Solo

I'm in the Burlingame Fred Meyer,
a paradise of useless trinkets.
I'm about to put a Revlon cream eye shadow
in my purse,
one that's close to the color of that MAC eye shadow
Tabitha chose for me that day in Nob Hill.
I glance around to see if anyone's watching.
It's not that I'm scared
or I've been rehabilitated by
Shawn and her stupid program—
even though some of the stuff she says makes sense—
it just seems weird now
to steal on your own,
especially when what you steal
makes you think of other people.

Besties

The yearbook is officially closed!
Rachelle announces.
Everyone claps except Dustin Diaz,
who looks like he may be on his last leg of love.
I gather all my stuff as Rachelle high-fives everyone.
I envy her.
She has her place in the world
and this is it.

Congratulations, I say to her. *You did an
   awesome job.*
She gives me a tight smile.
She's the girl who called me her bestie
for a few months or so,
even though it would never make the final edit.

*Did you see that photo of you
and Tabitha Foster and Maureen Truax?* she asks.
In the "Friends Forever" section?
The way she says it is snide and strange.
I'd be careful of Maureen, she adds.
I saw her steal Ms. Hoberman's Romeo and
   Juliet *program.*
*She took it right off the desk when she thought no
   one saw.*
I told Principal Prescott and he's pissed.
If this were the play *Romeo and Juliet,*

Rachelle would be in the role of the apothecary;
she relishes selling poison to people.
I plaster a smile on my face
and walk out, pretending to taste
absolutely nothing at all.

*MOE

MAY 3

I had the dos and don'ts of shoplifting written down, but when it came time for me to actually steal something, I did it all wrong. I acted guilty. I stole from someone I know. I didn't make sure the coast was clear. But I wanted to prove to my friends I wasn't a phony. I couldn't think of anything better than a souvenir from the field trip, where we all should have been sitting with each other instead of off in our corners with other people, pretending to be strangers. That's what I was thinking as I sit here waiting to go into the principal's office, where everything is about to go even more wrong than it already is.

TABITHA

HATE MAIL

As I'm going to my locker right before sixth period, I make sure the path is free of all assholes first. That's when I see an envelope jammed into a slat of my locker. As I'm about to pull it out, I hear:

"Hey, Tabitha."

I jump. I can't help it. I turn to see Brady standing there.

"What'd you get?" he drawls, pointing to the envelope.

I give him a tight smile and shrug.

"I hope it isn't hate mail," he says, pushing his hair out of his eyes. I try not to notice his biceps, other than the fact that they no longer appeal to me.

"Then here, you do the honors." If it's hate mail, it might as well be opened by someone I hate.

He rips it open, then reacts. "What the hell? Did *you*

steal this?" he cackles, holding up the contents of the envelope.

"No!" I say.

"Then why the hell do you have it?"

I yank it out of his hand.

"Is that, like, a gift from Patrick Cushman?"

I roll my eyes. Seriously? This is what he wants to harass me over?

"What are you talking about, Brady?" I give him a flat look.

"I saw you eating lunch with him the other day." He glowers as Taryn walks up.

"Hi, sweetie," Taryn purrs to me. "I love your shoes."

She and Brady meet eyes. I look back and forth between the two of them.

"We didn't do anything," Taryn blurts, guilty as shit. Brady gives her a sharp look, and I see everything laid out. Brady is now hooking up with my so-called best friend. And even though she feels bad about it, she's fine sacrificing our friendship for it. Not that I blame her. There wasn't much to our relationship anyway, besides fashion and gossip and jealousy.

"You guys are so gross," I say.

Brady steps forward, reaching out for me—it's hard to tell if he's trying to comfort me or hurt me, but I do the thing that I probably should have done a long time ago. As hard as I can, I kick him in the balls.

"FUCK!" he shouts.

"What the hell?!" Taryn screeches.

I wish I could say I kicked him hard enough to make

him fall over, but to be honest, leg strength isn't really my forte.

"You're such a bitch," Brady says as he leans against the lockers, trying to catch his breath.

"I really hate that word," I snarl, and walk away, tucking the Shakespeare program under my arm. People are staring at me as I go, probably because they agree with Brady's assessment that I am not so nice. But you know what? There are people whose opinions matter to me, and these aren't them.

MAY 4

To the Parent/Guardian of Maureen Truax:

This is notification that Maureen Truax is being considered for suspension in accordance with Oregon Statutes 120.13(1)(B)(3) for a period of 5 days from May 3—May 10.

Maureen Truax is under suspension consideration because she:

*Violated or refused to comply with school or district rules as stated in the code of conduct.

More specifically, she is being accused of stealing the personal property of Ms. Janette Hoberman.

Enclosed are materials encouraging your child to enroll in Shoplifters Anonymous, a local rehabilitation program that specializes in this problem.

If you choose to appeal this consideration, you must communicate your appeal, in writing, to the District Administrator within 5 days following the commencement of the investigation as stated in the Board Policy MTL.

Students who have been suspended shall not be denied the opportunity to take any quarterly, semester, or grading period examinations missed during the suspension period or to complete course work missed during the suspension period.

Prior to reinstatement, School Board policy requires that one or both parents (guardians) accompany your child to school for a readmittance conference with the principal. If you have any questions regarding this matter, please call me at 503.555.0188.

Sincerely,

Gerard Prescott

Gerard Prescott
Principal

More Buried Treasure

In Geometry 2,
Noah Simos leans over and says to me,
I think someone's trying to get your attention.
He points to Tabitha
through the classroom window.
Noah looks confused. *You guys are friends?*
Depends on the day, I say
before getting a bathroom pass
from Mrs. Klein
and heading out into the hallway.

I heard Moe took the Shakespeare program, I blurt
right when I walk up to Tabitha.
Yeah, well, if she did, Tabitha says,

only one person has proof.

She holds up Ms. Hoberman's prized possession,

the *Romeo and Juliet* program

with all fourteen cast members' names scrawled on
   it in ink.

Even the one with the boner.

TABITHA

SUSTAINABLE

I'm looking at Patrick Cushman's Facebook, trying to think of what to message him, when my mom knocks on the bedroom door.

"We're going to sushi," she says, which is kind of a shock because we used to go all the time until a year ago, when my dad was convinced he had mercury poisoning. He never really did, but he poisoned my mom with paranoia, which might be worse than mercury poisoning.

She drives us to Bamboo Sushi, which is on the east side. She likes it because it's "sustainable sushi," which must mean that all the fish are, like, free-range. Although when I asked her about it, she informed me that free-range fish do not actually exist. The place has all this art on the walls, and there's this big frame filled with hundreds of white origami swans all lined up perfectly. If you look at it from a distance, they make their own pattern, but if you get close, you can see they're just rows and rows of folded white paper. We sit at the back of the restaurant at the sushi bar, an L-shaped wide plank of wood lined with little tea lights. The sushi chef hands us a plate of albacore carpaccio with pickled shiitakes. I don't really like it, but it's one of my mom's favorites. He asks her if she'd like to try one of their signature sake flights.

"No, thanks. I'll have a green tea," she says.

"Mom, come on," I say, rolling my eyes. "Are you trying to prove a point by ordering tea?"

"No, I'm ordering it because I want to," she says.

"Whatever." I'm not sure whether to believe her.

After she gets her tea and takes a sip, she says, "I'm starting a program like you did."

I look at her, surprised.

"AA," she continues. "It helped you, didn't it?"

"I guess...." I trail off, not exactly wanting to admit that Shoplifters Anonymous was pretty useless when it came to curing my shoplifting.

"You can't tell people what to do," she says. "But sometimes you can inspire them toward a better path of action. You did that for me."

She clinks her tea with my glass of water, and I don't know what to say other than that I'm not sure when my mom became all Buddha and that raw fish never tasted so good.

*MOE

MAY 5

Principal Prescott called Aunt B to say my suspension was lifted because Ms. H's program had been found and turned in by two students. He added that even though the theft is going to be taken off my permanent record, I still might have to attend a rehabilitation program. Hilarious.

Aunt B was relieved and happy, but not so happy we got to go out to Zeppo for dinner or anything. Marc asked Aunt B if the principal told her who the two students were who turned in the program. She said no, but I said to Marc, "I'm pretty sure you can guess, can't you?" I couldn't tell what he was thinking, but we just left it at that and went to play some Rage.

Mutual Comprehension

My dad is on the phone
when I walk past his office,
but he hangs up
and calls out to me, *Today's your last day of that class,*
isn't it?
I back up and nod yes.
Can I drive you? he asks.
Sure, I say.

He gets up and strides over to me.
I have no idea what's coming
until he puts an arm around me and says,
You're doing okay, kiddo.
I'm not exactly sure what he means
and maybe one day I'll figure it out

or maybe I won't;
he is a fifty-year-old man, after all,
and I'm a sixteen-year-old girl,
so we're not exactly built for mutual comprehension.

He hugs me close
and it's a little awkward,
so he lets go abruptly
and walks back to his desk.
I say bye
and we smile at each other for a second,
two people who were always tied
together by one person,
who, try as she might,
just couldn't seem to stay.

Gift

When I walk into class,
Moe's already sitting in the back,
hoodie up around her head,
boots splayed out in front of her.
When she sees me,
she looks up like an owl
peeking out,
big dark eyes
that could either cut you
or warm you
and right now it's somewhere in between.

The Final Share

Tabitha arrives five minutes late for class,
but still in time to see Gina give her testimonial
complete with iPhone photos
of every relative she's ever met
and every pet she's ever owned
and every feeling she's ever had
because apparently her life has been so changed
by Shoplifters Anonymous
that she needs to share
extra hard today.
She finally stops
and Shawn asks if anyone has anything else to say.
Moe stands up
and Tabitha and I look at each other, surprised.
Before Moe starts to talk,
Shawn asks her if she can take off her hoodie, please.
She does and her hair spills out;
it's no longer cherry red but kind of a sandy blond.
It looks like a natural color if
I had any clue what her natural color might be.

A few months ago
I was walking out of the supermarket
next to a little old lady who was stealing a pack of bologna
and a pair of rubber gloves.
The sensor went off
and they grabbed me instead of her.

I told them I didn't take anything,
but they didn't believe me.
When they couldn't find anything on me,
they asked me if I knew who stole.
I figured the old lady had it worse than I did,
so I said no.
I needed a distraction from waiting in my room
for a guy who doesn't show up
or hanging out with people who will get me into trouble,
so I came here
and figured I'd come once or twice,
but then I met some people....
She looks over at Tabitha and me.
...And I decided maybe there were
other reasons to stay.

Shawn runs up and hugs her
and everyone claps and thanks her for sharing.
and Gina decides now would be a good time to cry.
Moe sits down abruptly
and looks over at Tabitha and me and mouths,
Can we go to the Roxy now?

*MOE

MAY 6

After Shawn signed our forms saying we'd successfully completed Shoplifters Anonymous, the three of us went to eat Quentin Tarantunas to celebrate. I teased Elodie about going to Spring Fling with my brother and she blushed. It was obvious she's totally in love with him. I don't understand love. It makes zero sense. Friendships are a little easier I guess. Maybe it helps if you meet in a totally weird support group for people who are trying to "fill the hole inside," to quote Shawn.

There are still three weeks of junior year left, then one more year of high school, and then we graduate and grow up and go to college and get married and have babies and live out the rest of our lives. I don't know what's going to happen next, but as long as we keep eating Quentin Tarantunas together, it seems like a pretty good start.

Now What

After we eat, this is normally the part
where we all split up,
go steal stuff,
and meet to compare the spoils.
But it doesn't seem right now.

So we walk to the MAX together
and hop aboard,
heading to buy stuff for real this time,
with the Nordie's gift certificate my dad gave me.

Our bags aren't going to end up full of loot,
but when you've scored as much as we've
    scored,
taking more just seems like overkill.

TABITHA

THE PHONE CALL

When I walk in, my mom tells me Brady called. He's been sending me texts for the past few days. I've been ignoring them.

"I don't want to talk to him," I say.

"Sometimes it's better to have a difficult conversation than to avoid one," she says. Did I mention she started going to AA last week?

"Fine." I take the phone out of her hand and dial.

"Hey, babe," Brady answers. On the first ring, no less.

"Sorry I kicked you," I apologize. He may not be the greatest guy on planet Earth, but I'll sleep easier knowing I've said I'm sorry.

He chuckles. "Yeah, well, maybe I deserved it."

"Why do you keep calling me?" I ask, itching to be done with this conversation.

"I want us to go together tomorrow night," he says.

"What?" Is he seriously saying this?

"Spring Fling. Let's do it. We planned on it, so I think we should still go."

"What about Taryn?"

"She's a little too fucked up for my taste." Nice. I can only imagine the things he's said about *me* to Taryn. "You still there?" he asks after a second.

"Yeah, but..." I pause, thinking it through before adding, "I'm not going anywhere with you. Ever." I hear him inhale sharply, sucking air through his perfect mouth. With that, I hang up.

Downstairs, I find my mom sitting in the kitchen, peeling an orange.

"How'd it go?" she asks.

"He said we should go to Spring Fling together."

"And...?" She pours herself a glass of Pellegrino and adds a little juice from the orange to it.

"I said no."

"Well, you don't have to go with a date, do you? You can go with your friends."

I shrug. We sit there for a second. Then I say, "I told him I didn't want to see him again."

"Okay, okay," she says. After a minute she adds, "I did too."

"You told who that?" I'm confused.

"Your dad. Jeffrey's filing the divorce papers on Monday."

I sit there, too shocked to even speak.

"I thought for a long time he was the love of my life." She looks down at her hands, ashamed.

"Well, he was, right?" I ask.

"Not really. You are." She smiles at me, trying not to cry. I try not to cry too, but then I tell myself at a certain point, it's okay if you do.

MAY 7

Aunt B and Marc and I were in the middle of dinner when the doorbell rang. It was Noah. He said, "Can I talk to your aunt, please?" My aunt came out, and he said without even looking at me, "Hey, Ms. Danner, I was wondering if I could take Maureen to the Spring Fling, if that's okay with you?" My aunt was like, "If you're not proposing marriage, then I think it's fine if you just ask her yourself." Then she left the room and I was just kind of standing there and he looked at me and said, "Well?" I shrugged yes and he said something about picking me up on Saturday at seven. I said, "Are you sure you can be seen in public with me?" and hadn't he been talking about going with Kayla Lee? He said he didn't have anything in common with her, not that she was a bad person or anything, but the other day in Geometry 2 he saw two girls who he would have never guessed in a million years hung out together and it made him realize you never know who your friends could be. Then Marc walked by and whistled at us and I think Noah got embarrassed and I told Marc to shut the hell up before I punched him and Noah kissed me really fast on the cheek and left. I ran to my room and that's where I'm writing this now.

Elodie

A Necessary Evil

I'm putting on Revlon eye shadow
and Jenna is trying to tell me
about some prom she went to when she was my age
and it's a really long story
that involves ruffles and
a foreign-exchange student named Karl.
Thank God the doorbell rings.
I open the door, and there's Tabitha.
Okay, bye! I say to Jenna.
We're going to get dressed at Tabitha's house.
I grab Tabitha's arm and try to rush out,
but Jenna says, *What's that?*, pointing to the red dress
over Tabitha's arm.
It's for Elodie. I got it from Betsey Johnson, Tabitha says.
No way! I say. I can't believe it.

Wait! Jenna blurts. *I have the perfect thing to go with it!*
She dashes upstairs
and Tabitha looks at me. *Whoa. High energy.*
I shrug. *She eats a lot of kale.*

Jenna runs back downstairs with a silver necklace
and hands it to me, all proud.
It's got a big, sparkly pendant
and it's something my mom would never have worn,
but then again, my mom wasn't super stylish.
Ooh, I love it, Tabitha says
as Jenna fastens it around my neck.
She tells me I look beautiful
and maybe she isn't half wrong.
She takes a picture of us as Tabitha and I walk out,
to show my dad when he gets home later,
and before we go, I stop and say,
Thanks for the necklace,
and Jenna grins, really happy,
until Tabitha adds: *Don't worry.*
Even though she's a shoplifter,
I'll make sure she gives it back.

*MOE

MAY 11

Noah arrived at exactly 6:50 to get me. He wore a black suit with a blue tie. It didn't exactly match my purple dress, but that's okay. He gave me a flower bouquet instead of a corsage, which is cool, because having a clump of flowers on your wrist all night seems annoying. I got him a red rose boutonniere to wear. When he first saw me, he said, "WHOA. You look awesome." I felt like I couldn't stop smiling, even though it was for an idiotic tradition. And my aunt made us pose for pictures, a ton of them. She kept saying how proud she was of me. All I know is the lady has a thing for taking photos, but I also know I'm not going to regret having a keepsake or two.

TABITHA

TABITHA'S HOUSE

I take Elodie through the living room, which has stopped being redecorated for the time being. My mom "put the project on hold." Still, everything looks perfect. Lilies are on the mantel and in the kitchen. My dad never liked flowers because of his allergies, but now that he's moved out, they're everywhere.

"I love your house so much," Elodie sighs.

"We might not be here much longer."

"Really?" She's surprised.

"My parents are getting divorced."

"Wow." Elodie takes note of my face. "You okay?"

"Yeah," I say. "I am." And I mean it. Except for the fact that there is an annoyingly giant vase of dahlias on the bathroom counter that I have to move every time I brush my teeth, everything is exactly the way it should be.

*   *   *

When we get to my room, Elodie looks at all the piles of clothes and snow globes and frames and perfume bottles on the floor. "Is this all your loot?"

I nod. "I'm getting rid of some of it."

"Ooh—look how much good stuff there is," Elodie says, holding up a black winter coat with a white furry collar.

"I used to make lists of how much everything cost and then add it all up. Seeing the total made me happy. Now it just seems like meaningless numbers. Not to mention, it's crap I don't need."

"So no more stealing?" Elodie studies me.

I nod. "According to Jeffrey, the judge is accepting my plea bargain, but if I get caught again, it'll go on my record."

Elodie stands in the red dress in front of the closet, admiring herself in the full-length. She's not making any kind of Mirror Face as she does it. She just is who she is.

She turns and looks at me. "I've got to admit, though, I wouldn't love this dress half as much if it weren't stolen."

I hand her a pair of silver hoop earrings. "As long as you're wearing a stolen dress, you might as well complete the outfit."

Elodie takes them with a smile.

"Limo's here!" my mom calls from downstairs.

"What?!" Elodie and I look at each other, excited.

"It's an Ecolimo!" she calls up. "It runs on corn!"

Elodie laughs. "Your mom's awesome."

I nod in agreement. We gather up our stuff, put on lip gloss, and go to the Spring Fling.

Wallflower

Where once I would have felt like a wallflower,
loitering outside the bathroom,
now I'm a girl simply waiting for a friend.
Rachelle passes me with Dustin Diaz
and gives me the world's most pitying look.
But her pity doesn't have thorns anymore
because it doesn't exactly apply.

Out of the corner of my eye, I see Marc
and some of his friends walk in.
He's not really dressed up,
but somehow he's managed
to make himself even more handsome,
which makes Wallflower Me want to run and hide
because that's what wallflowers do.

I try to shrink out of his way
but it's pointless.

He stops right in front of me and says,
You look nice.
Thank you, I reply,
looking into his brown brown eyes.
I go from being an ordinary rhododendron
to a hot-pink dahlia,
from a former wallflower
to a blossom that's alive
in the world
again.

TABITHA

OLD FRIENDS

I come out of the bathroom stall and see Kayla at the sink putting on lip gloss. I almost bolt but then realize that would make me an asshole.

"Hey, Kayla," I wave awkwardly.

"Oh, hey," she says warily.

I quickly turn on the water, preparing to get out of there as quickly as possible. I pump soap into my palms. It's the kind that's made of sandy little granules that scratch your hands. So much for Spring Fling being a high-class event.

"Hey, Tabitha, I wanted to ask you something," Kayla says, stepping up next to me.

I know what's coming and I can't deal with it. I hold up a hand. "I don't want to gossip about Brady and Taryn or anybody else. If you're going to try to get in the middle of it, I'm sorry but I've got to go."

I turn to go, but she stops me. Oh God. This is going to be awkward and awful.

"Seriously, Kayla—"

"No—I just wondered..." She drops her voice. "Do you have a tampon?"

"A tampon?" I'm so confused.

"I just got my period. Can you believe it? Again! It's like I'm haunted by the god of menstruation or something." She waves a hand in front of her dress. "And I'm wearing white!"

I can't help it. I start laughing. She looks hurt for a second. "No, I'm sorry!" I say. "It's just—you're funny."

"I'm not funny. I'm bleeding!" she wails. "As if it weren't bad enough that Noah decided at the last minute to come with someone else. Spring Fling sucks!"

"Wait here," I say. "I'll go find something."

I pass Elodie, but she's so busy talking to Marc, she doesn't even notice. As I pass Keith Savage cuddling with Zoe Amato, I hear Zoe say, "What's Tabitha running around about?"

"Maybe she's having fun," Keith responds.

"I am, actually," I call back over my shoulder. They look at me kind of weird, but who cares? I beeline toward Ms. Hoberman, who is grooving on the sidelines to the band's fairly unpleasant cover of "Single Ladies (Put a Ring on It)." I whisper my request into Ms. Hoberman's ear and she says, "Oh, of course!" She got a degree in education to prepare for stuff like this.

"Oh, my gosh, thank you so much," I say as she digs through her purse.

"So, have you ever thought about writing for the school blog?" she asks as she roots around.

"Not really..."

"Well, you should. We need talented writers to contribute, even just once or twice a week. It can look good on a college application...?"

"I don't know...." I'm starting to get anxious. Why didn't I ask someone else for a tampon?

"You could even write under a pseudonym," she suggests.

I think about it for a second, then I realize, why not? What have I got to lose? And, more important, what have I got to hide?

"No, I could probably write it under my name," I say. "Yeah. I could totally do that."

She beams at me, then announces, "Ta-da!" and triumphantly pulls out an organic cotton tampon. I take it from her and run back to the bathroom, where I find Kayla at the sink, trying to fold a stack of paper towels into a panty-size bundle.

"Whoa, whoa, whoa," I say. "Use this. It's cruelty-free."

She snatches the tampon out of my hand, practically collapsing with relief.

"Oh my God, Tabs, thank you!" she says, exhaling and hugging me. "You saved my life."

"Anytime," I say with a smile.

She looks at me. "I've been wanting to ask you something."

"What?"

"You're into Patrick Cushman, aren't you?"

I don't answer.

"Well, for the record, I think he's really nice. And weirdly superhot," she says with a genuine smile. "You should go for it."

"Really?" I'm shocked. And not totally opposed.

She gives me a thumbs-up and I head out of the bathroom, realizing that sometimes all it takes to reunite old friends—maybe not forever, but at least for a night—is a chance encounter, a dose of advice, and a tiny piece of feminine protection.

*MOE

MAY 12, 3:25 A.M.

At first the dance was kind of awkward, but fortunately we got a table where all five of us could sit. It's bizarre trying to make chitchat with everyone on their best behavior. Especially when one of the people is your brother. But then fortunately he broke the ice and told some stupid story about the time in junior high I dislocated his elbow when we were wrestling, which seemed to make everyone laugh. Noah leaned over and said, "That's so you," and I guess he's right. But now, being in a dress at a dance is me too. Who says you can't be both?

The best part of the night was when the DJ announced he was playing a slow song "that goes out to Maureen, from Tabitha and Elodie." I was like, WHAT? And then the song came on—"Glory of Love" by Peter Cetera. Tabs and Elodie elbowed Noah like they'd sort of planned it.

Noah grabbed my hand and took me out on the dance floor, which was pretty empty because the entire student body obviously doesn't understand the joy of a cheesy love song. We started slow dancing and I told him that this was one of my parents' favorite jams, and he said that was cool.

Tabitha came out with Patrick Cushman. It wasn't as if suddenly they were a couple or anything, but they kept giggling like they were into each other. As for Marc and Elodie, at first I thought it would be creepy to dance next to my brother and his "girlfriend," but he kept some distance so it wouldn't be weird. Plus, I made note of his ridiculous dance moves so as to mock him later. Tabitha and Elodie and I started mock-singing along to the lyrics, and some people looked confused, like for the first time they were the ones who didn't get the joke.

Later we did the Robot and the Running Man, and then it was over and we drove home. Noah asked me if I wanted to stop and get a hamburger. For a second I thought I wouldn't want to eat in front of him and then I realized we've lived next door to each other for six years so who cares. Plus, I was starving. After burgers, we went home and he walked me to the door and kissed me with hamburger breath on the front steps. I waited in my room for about ten minutes, thinking he was probably going to try to sneak in my window, but then he sent me a text: NIGHT C U TOMORROW. I wrote back OK and was really scared he had a terrible time, but he wrote: I MISS U. C U FOR BREAKFAST? It almost made me cry, even though I wish he was here right now so we could be together all night long. But I'm so tired, so I guess sleep is a good idea.

XOXOXOXO

New and Old

The yearbooks came out today
and everyone is busy looking through the pages
trying to find themselves.

I've been here nine months
and I'm more old than new now.
I'm old enough to know that Moe Truax
has a soft spot for *The Golden Girls*.
I'm old enough to know that Marc Truax
is as good at physics as he is at wheelies.
I'm old enough to know that Tabitha Foster
can't tell a joke to save her life,
but it doesn't make her any less funny.
I'm new enough to have only recently figured out

that people never stop surprising you,
even if they're your best friends.

As I walk out the front door of school,
I see Tabitha and Moe waiting for me in the parking lot.
We're taking Tabitha's new car to the Roxy,
the shiny silver Prius her dad bought her
to make himself feel better
about finally packing up and going,
the car she accepted with a smile
and moved on,
because she's smart enough to know you can't make
    people—
especially your parents—
become who you wish they were.

The sun starts out of the clouds
and finds its way to Tabitha's hair
as she slides behind the wheel.
It's hair that girls like me will probably
envy forever, whether we're friends or foes.
Moe sits shotgun, her feet up on the dash,
wiggling her toes,
which she's painted neon turquoise
so they looked like little blue Smurf turds.

The yearbooks came out today
and everyone is busy looking through the pages

trying to find themselves.
I don't need to.
It took me a minute,
but I already know
where I am.

TABITHA

HOARDERS

"*Hoarders* called," Moe says to me. "They want to do an entire season on you."

She's staring in awe as Elodie and I unload gobs and gobs of stuff from the trunk of my car. We've just pulled up in front of the women's homeless shelter on Burnside. We decided to take all the stuff we've ever stolen and donate it to homeless people. Okay, that's a lie. Not *all* of it. Maybe half. It was Elodie's idea. I think she wanted to show Marc she wasn't an evil person and that she was a good influence on his sister and all. Noted.

"I like this," Elodie says, holding up a pink pencil skirt. "Can I keep it?"

"Sorry," I say. "Doreen's eyeballing it." I point to a really pretty but really skinny lady with a crazy mane of brown hair who's watching us.

We haul the stuff up the steps to the shelter, and Moe's right. Based on this much stuff, we clearly should have been professional thieves. Maybe all this time we should have been planning a bank robbery instead of just ripping off stores. Oh well. Next year.

Elodie has boxes full of books and scarves and makeup and knickknacks. As for me, I have boxes and boxes of clothes. I even put a couple of dolls and two of my snow globes in there for good measure. I figured if some of the women have kids, they'll like them.

"Hey, girls, I'm Natalie," says a friendly black lady who lets us into the shelter. "Shawn said you might be coming by."

I look at Elodie, surprised. "You told Shawn we were coming?"

Elodie shrugs. "I figured she'd know the best place to donate."

"Getting that phone call probably made her entire life," Moe says, grabbing a Gumby doll out of my box and holding it up with a quizzical look. "Why you no keep Gumby?"

I swat Moe with it as Natalie leads us into the entryway of the shelter, which obviously isn't the world's most cheerful place, and then guides us around the corner to the main living area. She points out where to put down our stuff, and immediately a group of women descends on the goods.

"Dolce and Gabbana? Wuh-what?" says a woman in her twenties with a gap in her teeth, holding up a jacket to her friend. I wince. I love that jacket. I remember when I stole it at Mario's and wore it every day that winter. I wish I could keep it. Suddenly, I wish I could keep all this stuff.

As I'm thinking this, "Doreen" steps up, holding the pink skirt and a white shirt with big cuffs. "Is this really Prada?" she asks shyly.

"Yeah," I confirm. "Well, last season."

She pulls the shirt on over her tank top, and it falls to the perfect length on her hips. It accents her collarbone just right. So *that's* how it's supposed to look.

"Wow. It looks way better on you than it ever did on me," I say, genuinely impressed.

"Really?" She beams. "I've never worn anything like this."

"Well, you look amazing."

As I watch her head off with her new outfit, Moe snaps a photo of me with her phone. "*Hoarders* would be so proud."

I smack her, and Elodie laughs. Just then Natalie comes over. "Thanks, you guys, for coming by."

"Sure," Elodie says.

"If you ever have any more donations, you know where to find us."

"Let's hope we won't," Elodie says. "We're trying to reform ourselves."

We say good-bye and walk outside. It's a perfect sunny day in Portland, the first real summer moment of the year. It's times like this, when you're hit with greenery and blue sky, that you realize maybe all those months of rain really do pay off. As I walk down the steps with Moe and Elodie, I'm glad we gave away our stuff. Stolen trinkets lead you to places you never predicted you'd go, but eventually you have to leave them behind.

ACKNOWLEDGMENTS

Thanks to:

Gibran Perrone, for your keen eye and brilliant ideas.

Kate Sullivan, the editrix with the most cake. You saved this book's life.

Steven Malk, because if every writer had a representative like you, the world would be a happier place.

Pam Garfinkel, for reading and rereading.

Seth Jaret, did you ever know that you're my hero?

Rushie Coughran, for your Portland savvy and ongoing awesomeness.

Mel and Katie, for being the best parents ever.

Tavi Gevinson, for setting the bar so high.

Petra Collins, who brought her gorgeous vision to the cover.

Isla Cowan and Ali Harcourt, for their cover model prowess.

Kelly Abeln, for setting the design stage.

Gerry Huffman, for your exuberant, Diet Coke–fueled support in the wee, wee hours.

Jessica O'Toole, for being the most anal nerd I know.

Shannon Woodward, for lending constant peppiness to the world's smallest, surliest writer's group.

Lee Cohen, because nobody does it better.

Ashley Kruythoff, for being a human ball of sunshine.

Leslie Shumate, for her expert author hand-holding.

Tracy and Mimi Underwood, for their geographical know-what.

Olivia Baird and all the Chimacum girls, for reading this book, and the hometown librarians, for supporting it.

Alene Moroni, for being a trinket I can't live without.

Katy Perry, for all the dance parties you inspired.

Kurt Lustgarten, for being the man of my teenage dreams.